For Susan –

Lee Bennett Hopkins
2/88

Mama & Her Boys

Mama & Her Boys

Lee Bennett Hopkins

HARPER & ROW, PUBLISHERS

NEW YORK

Cambridge
Hagerstown
Philadelphia
San Francisco

London
Mexico City
São Paulo
Sydney

1817

Mama and Her Boys is a work of fiction. All names, characters, and events are fictitious, and any resemblance to real persons or actual events is unintentional.

MAMA AND HER BOYS
Copyright © 1981 by Lee Bennett Hopkins
All rights reserved. No part of this book may be used or reproduced in any manner whatsoever without written permission except in the case of brief quotations embodied in critical articles and reviews. Printed in the United States of America. For information address Harper & Row, Publishers, Inc., 10 East 53rd Street, New York, N.Y. 10022. Published simultaneously in Canada by Fitzhenry & Whiteside Limited, Toronto.
First Edition

Library of Congress Cataloging in Publication Data
Hopkins, Lee Bennett.
  Mama and her boys.

  SUMMARY: When a boy interviews a custodian for his school newspaper, friendship ensues, and a family gains a father.
  [1. Remarriage—Fiction. 2. Mothers and sons—Fiction] I. Title.
PZ7.H7754Man 1981   [Fic]   81-47445
ISBN 0-06-022578-5   AACR2
ISBN 0-06-022579-3 (lib. bdg.)

DEDICATION

To:

Misha Arenstein
Charles John Egita
Marilyn E. Marlow
&
Charlotte Zolotow
A to Z—for me.
LBH

1

"Mama remembers everything."

The telephone rang.

"I'll get it," Chris told Mark, running from their bedroom into the kitchen. "Hello," he said, answering the phone. "This is Christopher Hugh Kipness, here."

"What's the matter with you?" Mama quickly, briskly asked. "Don't you think I know who you are? Don't you know this is me on the telephone?"

"I know it's you now, Mama," Chris said, "but I didn't know it was you when the phone rang. You told me always to say hello and give my name—my full name—whenever I answer the phone. Don't you remember, Mama?"

1

"Of course I remember. Mama remembers everything. Every single thing. But you *don't* have to say all that when *I* call. I'm a little busy, son, so do me a favor and put your brother on the phone. I want to tell him something."

"O.K., Mama. He's in the bedroom. I'll get him."

"Good. Go get him. Is everything all right at home?"

"Yes, everything's just fine, Mama. Hold on a second and I'll get Mark."

He put the receiver down and ran back into their bedroom. "Mark, Mama's on the phone."

"What does she want?" Mark asked.

"I don't know. She just said she wanted to talk to you. She sounds a little cranky, so you'd better hurry up."

Mark dashed from the bedroom into the kitchen.

"Hello, Mama. It's Mark."

"You know? Sometimes I think I'm going crazy. How many sons do I have. Two, right? You and your little brother. When I called he told me his name. Now you're telling me yours. Don't you think I know your names by now? Wasn't I the one who gave you your names when you were born? As a matter of fact I named you, Mark Charles, *before* you were born."

Mark knew better than to answer. Tuesday was always a busy day for her at the laundry and she was probably a little tired. He remained

2

silent. It didn't take longer than a second for her to start up again.

"The reason I called is that I want you and your little brother to come down to the laundry at six fifteen. I'm taking you out to eat tonight at the Burger Barn."

"Tonight?" Mark asked.

"Didn't I just say tonight?"

"Yes, Mama, but we never eat out on Tuesday night."

"Well *this* Tuesday night we are. Meet me at six fifteen, here at the laundry."

"O.K., Mama," Mark said. "We'll be there at six fifteen. Mama, is everything all right?"

"Of course everything is all right. Everything's just fine and dandy. The reason I want to go out for supper is that I want to tell you both something—something very interesting. And I want to talk with you and Christopher Hugh about it over dinner at the Burger Barn, you hear?"

"I hear, Mama. We'll be at the laundry at six fifteen."

"Son, before you come, stop up at Mrs. Rand's apartment and ask her if she needs anything. I didn't have time to call her today. Since we'll be downtown, there might be something we can pick up for her."

"I will, Mama."

"Good-bye, now. I've got to go. I have a lot of laundry to do before the store closes. I'll see you later, son. Close the windows before you leave, just in case it rains."

"I will, Mama."

"Oh, and make sure you and Christopher Hugh wash up nice before you come. I don't want you to have to use the public toilets at the Burger Barn. 'Bye again."

" 'Bye, Mama," Mark said, hanging up the telephone. "Chris!" he called.

"Yes?"

"Mama wants us to meet her at the laundry at six fifteen. We're going to eat supper at the Burger Barn."

"Yeah!" he shouted. "I love the Burger Barn. I'm going to have a Double Barnburger Special with melted cheese and pickles on top."

"I don't understand why we're going out to eat on a Tuesday night. The only night we ever eat out is on Saturday," said Mark.

"Who cares?" Chris replied. "I could eat a Double Barnburger Special with melted cheese and pickles on top every night of the week. I love them. Maybe Mama's too tired to cook to-night."

"That's not the reason. I know it isn't. Mama said she had something interesting—very inter-esting—to talk about. Usually when she wants to talk with us about something interesting, it means she's going to get a new job."

"Do you think she's going to quit her job at Mr. Jacobs' Laundry, Mark? Mama likes to get

4

new jobs. Maybe that's what's interesting."

Mark didn't answer, but said to himself, "That's exactly what I'm afraid of!"

He silently prayed she wasn't going to leave Mr. Jacobs' Laundry. Mama seemed very happy with her work. She liked the freedom Mr. Jacobs gave her, and even liked Mr. Jacobs.

"This is one of the best jobs I've ever had," Mama often said. "Mr. Jacobs has lived up to all his promises. He's a man of his word. There aren't too many men, especially bosses, who live up to promises. Most bosses promise you all kinds of things, and once you start working for them, they treat you like trash. Like they own you.

"I have Mondays off. I almost run the place myself, and I do all our laundry free. He doesn't even charge me for the liquid detergent or bleach. The pay's good too. Mama was lucky to get this job. Lucky, indeed!"

The pay was good. Mama was even able to buy everything for cash at George's Grocery Store instead of running up bills from week to week.

She can't quit again, Mark thought. She can't!

"Want to play a game of Old Maid with me before we go?" Chris asked. "We've got time."

"No," Mark said. "I have two pages of fractions to do for homework. The only thing I hate about fifth grade is the math.

"Chris, Mama asked me to go upstairs to see if Mrs. Rand needs anything from downtown.

Do you want to come up with me?"

"Sure. I'll bring my deck of Old Maid with me. Maybe she feels like playing."

"Don't ask her to play again," Mark said. "You told me she played two games with you this afternoon."

"And lost both." Chris giggled.

"That's another reason for not bothering her. How would you feel if you lost all the time?"

"I wouldn't feel anything because I never lose."

"Leave the Old Maid alone for now. I'm only going to ask her a quick question. Come on."

They walked up the familiar, gray-steel stairs to Mrs. Rand's apartment and knocked on the door.

"Who's there?" she called.

"It's me, Mrs. Rand. Mark."

"And Chris, too!" Chris added.

Opening the door, Mrs. Rand said, "What a nice surprise. My two favorite boys are here. Come on in."

Instead of dashing in the way they usually did, Mark and Chris stood still and looked at her, at one another, and at her again. They were surprised to see her standing in her well-worn, faded-blue bathrobe with her long, white hair let down. It was the first time they had ever seen her like this.

"Are you sick, Mrs. Rand?" Chris blurted out.

"Sick? What gives you that idea, son? I'm as

6

healthy as a young bear leavin' his lair for the first time after sleepin' all winter long."

"Your hair is beautiful," Mark said. "It's so long. I never knew you had such long hair."

"Me either," Chris said, gazing at her hair flowing down way past her shoulders. "How do you get it all back up on your head?"

"If you come on in, I'll tell you. You don't have to stand in the doorway. Come on in."

Closing the door, she asked, "What's on your minds?"

"Your hair's on my mind," Chris said. "You look so different."

"I just washed it," she said. "My hair's been this long since I was a young girl. I always wear it pinned up in a bun 'cause it's easier. When it dries, all I have to do is pin it back up—one, two, three—then it's not in my way all the time. Now tell me what you came up for."

"Mama called," Mark said. "We're meeting her for dinner and she wanted to know if you needed anything from downtown."

"Bless her soul!" Mrs. Rand exclaimed. "That woman is always thinkin' about other people. When God made your mama, he threw away the mold. She's the only woman like her in this entire world. There's nothin' I need, but you thank her for thinkin' of me. Do either of you want a glass of milk or somethin'?"

"No, thank you," Mark replied.

"Chris?"

"No, thanks, Mrs. Rand. I have to save room in my stomach for the Burger Barn. That's where Mama's taking us."

"We have to go," Mark said. "I have some math homework to do before we meet Mama."

"Then you'd better run along. Schoolwork's important. I'll see you both tomorrow."

"Will your hair be still down?" Chris asked.

"No, it won't! My! I never thought my hair bein' down would cause such a reaction in you two. You tickle me pink. Remember to thank your mama for thinkin' of me. Good-bye, boys."

"Good-bye, Mrs. Rand," they echoed.

On their way to the laundry Chris said, "I can't believe how long her hair is, can you, Mark? She looks like a different person."

Mark didn't answer.

"Mark," Chris said, nudging his arm. "I'm talking to you."

"I'm sorry. I was thinking about something," he said.

"I was talking about Mrs. Rand's hair."

"You've talked enough about that already. Let's just walk together quietly. I'd like to think."

"Want to play step-on-the-cracks with me?"

"No," Mark answered.

"How about skip-a-sidewalk then?"

"No, I don't want to play anything. I said I'd like to think."

8

"Can't you think while you're playing a simple game?"

"Chris, please! I don't want to play anything. Just be still, please?"

He didn't want to talk or play a sidewalk game. His head was filled with thoughts of Mama.

After they had walked a few more blocks, Chris asked, "You finished thinking yet? We only have two blocks to go. If you're finished thinking, maybe we can play skip-a-sidewalk the rest of the way."

"O.K.," Mark said, giving in to him as he usually did. "Let's play. We'll get to the laundry faster that way."

2

*"Sometimes there are times
to ask questions."*

When they arrived at the laundry, Mr. Jacobs
was standing behind the cash register counting
the day's profits.

"Hi, Mr. Jacobs," Mark said.

"Oh, hello, Mark. Hello Chris," he called, lift-
ing his glasses from his face, placing them on
top of his balding head.

"Hi, Mr. Jacobs," Chris said. "Where's
Mama?"

"She's downstairs washing up."

"I thought she'd be finished work by now,"
Chris said. "We're going to eat out tonight at
the Burger Barn. That's why we're meeting her
here."

10

"I know," said Mr. Jacobs. "Your mama told me. She is finished work. She's downstairs washing herself up," he said, smiling. "She'll be up in a minute. I'll tell her you're here."

Walking to the rear of the store, he yelled, "Trudy, the kids are here."

"Be right up," she called back.

"Nice weather, isn't it?" Mr. Jacobs asked.

"Real nice," Mark answered.

"Looks like we're going to have a pleasant springtime," added Mr. Jacobs.

"It looks that way," Mark said, not knowing what else to say. He really never knew what to say to Mr. Jacobs. He was glad Mama soon appeared from downstairs.

Chris ran to her and gave her a hug. "You look pretty, Mama," he said. "And you smell pretty, too."

"How are my *boys*?" Mama asked, nearly screaming out the word *boys*. "Did my *boys* have a good day at school today?"

"I had a good day, Mama," Mark answered, walking over to give her a kiss.

"Me, too," Chris said. "We made spring flowers out of colored tissue paper. Miss Turner always lets us do interestin' things."

"Interest*ing*," Mama corrected. "There's a *g* at the end of that word. Always pronounce your final g's."

"Mrs. Rand doesn't," Chris said.

"Never mind what Mrs. Rand does or doesn't

11

do. Mrs. Rand is set in her ways. Besides, she never had the chances that people growing up today have. She grew up in times when it wasn't as easy for someone to get a good education. You do just what I tell you to do and you'll grow up smart. Smarter than the President of the United States."

"That won't take much doing," joked Mr. Jacobs.

"That's not funny," Mama answered. "Regardless of what you or anyone else thinks about the President, you should respect him and his position. No President ever made it by being dumb—nor by dropping his final g's. My *boys* are going to learn things correctly. Don't my *boys* look fine, Mr. Jacobs?"

"They always look fine to me, Trudy."

"By the way, I don't call my boys *kids* anymore and I wish you wouldn't either. Kids are baby goats," she said, hugging Mark and Chris. "These are my *boys!*"

Mark now realized why she had been saying *boys* so loudly. Mama always had a reason for everything she did.

"Mama," Chris said, "Mrs. Rand had her hair down. It comes down way past her shoulders. Did you know that?"

"I never gave much thought to Mrs. Rand's hair, Christopher Hugh."

"I didn't either until I saw it. You have to ask her to show it to you someday. She has enough hair to cover ten heads!"

"That's the way it goes," Mr. Jacobs said, removing his glasses and stroking his shiny head. "Sometimes life isn't fair. Some people have too much hair and others don't have any."

"Maybe Mrs. Rand could lend you some of hers, Mr. Jacobs," Chris said. "She's very nice."

Mr. Jacobs laughed. "If it would work, I'd ask her. Believe me, I'd ask her."

Mark and Mama laughed, too.

"We'd better get going now," Mama said. "Off we go to the Burger Barn together. Good night, Mr. Jacobs. I'll see you bright and early in the morning."

"Good night, Trudy. And good luck. Good night, *boys,*" he said with a smile.

"*Boys* is right," Mama said, huddling them close to her, squeezing their shoulders. "These are two of the finest boys in the whole wide world."

Mark felt a little uncomfortable over Mama's fussing. Eager to leave the laundry, he said good night to Mr. Jacobs.

"Good night," added Chris.

"Oh, by the way, Trudy, remember what I told you. The bill at the Burger Barn is on me tonight. Just let me know what it comes to in the morning."

"Thank you, Mr. Jacobs, but that won't be necessary. I'll pay for my boys' dinner—and for mine. Good night, now."

" 'Bye all," Mr. Jacobs said.

Once outside the laundry, Mark asked, "What did he mean by 'good luck'? And why does he want to pay for our dinner?"

"Don't bombard me with too many questions right now. There'll be enough time to talk and ask questions over dinner."

"Yeah, besides, you hate questions, right Mama?" Chris asked. "You only like answers, right?"

"Sometimes there are times to ask questions. Like tonight. Tonight I'm going to tell you something and you can ask all the questions you want to ask. Are you both hungry?"

"I'm starved," Chris said. "I can't wait to get my teeth into a Double Barnburger Special with melted cheese and pickles on top."

"And you, Mark Charles?"

"I guess so," he answered, still pondering what she was up to and when she'd finally get around to telling them about it. Something was brewing in Mama's mind. He knew there was. He could feel it.

"Eat your food slower," Mama told Chris as he was devouring his Double Barnburger Special. "If you eat slower, it gives your stomach a better chance to digest the food. A healthy digestive system is important."

"Yes, Mama," Chris mumbled.

"Mama," Mark carefully asked, "when are you

14

going to tell us about the interesting thing you said you were going to talk about?"

"Let's all finish our Barnburgers first. We'll talk about that while we finish our chocolate shakes. You've been quiet tonight, Mark Charles. Why don't you talk about what you did in school today? Christopher Hugh said he made tissue-paper flowers. What did you do, son?"

"Nothing special, Mama."

"You don't have to do special things every day. Tell me about an *un*special thing you did."

"I don't really want to talk about school," he said.

"Well I do!" she answered. "Your school day is important to me. Dinnertime is the time to talk about our days. It's our time to share. Sharing makes us understand one another better. We're going to share our days even if they don't seem exciting. Now tell us something you did in school today."

Although Mark wanted to hear about her day first and what she was going to tell them, he knew she'd never get on with it if he didn't say something.

"Mrs. Cochrane is teaching us fractions, Mama. She gave us two pages of homework to do."

"Did you do it?" she asked.

"Yes, Mama. I finished it before I met you."

"Good. Now see, that's something special."

"Math is boring," Mark said. "I don't know

15

what's so special about learning fractions."

"Learning fractions may not seem special to you now, but it is special. Everything you learn is important. I didn't think fractions were important when I was learning them, either. That's the fun in learning new things and storing them up in your head. You never know when something will pop up that you learned a long time ago and need right at the moment. I use fractions every day. I'd be in plenty of trouble if I didn't know the difference between a *half* a cup of detergent and a *whole* cup of bleach. You can't work in a laundry without knowing fractions."

Since she had mentioned the laundry, Mark thought it was a good time to get her off the subject of school.

"Mama, do you still like your job?" he asked.

"Of course I do. It's one of the best jobs I've ever had. I meet lots of nice people at the laundry. And Mr. Jacobs is very pleasant to me. Sometimes I feel like I own the place and Mr. Jacobs is working for me. That's a funny twist, isn't it? Mr. Jacobs told me I'm the best worker he's ever had except for his poor wife, may she rest in peace. He jokes about it. He tells me I'm the best thing that happened to the laundry business since the invention of liquid detergent."

Turning to Chris, she said, "Christopher Hugh, I *said* to eat that Barnburger slower. And

16

be careful not to get ketchup on your clean shirt."

"What's the joke?" Chris asked.

"What joke?" said Mama.

"About liquid detergent. I don't get the joke."

"Before liquid detergent was invented, people had to wash their clothes with soap powder and the soap powder used to get stuck in the washing machine and block it all up. Liquid detergent just mixes in with the water. It's safer for the washing machine and it does a better job on the clothes."

"I still don't get the joke," Chris said.

"Forget about it!" Mama snapped. "Some things are only funny between the people who think they are funny. Why did you ask me if I still like my job, Mark Charles?"

"I was just wondering, that's all, Mama."

"He was wondering if you were going to quit," Chris said.

Mark could have killed him.

"What? Quit? Where would you ever get such an idea?" she asked. "I just told you how much I like the job."

Mark was relieved to know that the interesting thing didn't mean a new job. But he was more curious than ever to know what she was going to tell them. He couldn't wait for Chris to finish eating. The next few minutes seemed to drag on endlessly.

"I'm through," Chris announced, wiping his

hands with a paper napkin. "Mama, can I have a Cheery Cherry Pie for dessert?"

"You know how I feel about those things," she answered. "They're junk."

"But look at all the cherries in them," he said, pointing to a poster. "I thought fruit was supposed to be good for you. You told us that."

"Fruit is good for you. Cherries are good fruits—real cherries. But the cherries in that stuff are all faked up—filled with chemicals and fake flavoring to make them taste like real cherries. Don't let that sign fool you, either. There are more cherries in that picture than any baker could fit into any one pie. Why, if they put even half of those cherries in the pie, the pie would be so heavy you wouldn't be able to lift it up from the counter.

"On the way home we can stop in Mrs. Kowalski's Bake Shop and you can have a chocolate-chip cookie. Mrs. Kowalski's chocolate-chip cookies are the best in town. She has a good reputation. She uses real ingredients in the stuff she bakes—not fake. How does that sound?"

"O.K., Mama," Chris answered. "A chocolate-chip cookie from Mrs. Kowalski's is better than nothing at all, I guess."

"You guessed right," Mama said.

"I'm finished, too, Mama," said Mark. "Can we talk now?"

"Yes, we should talk now. But I want you both to listen carefully and don't interrupt me until

18

I'm through. What I'm going to tell you is very important. After I tell you, you both can talk and ask as many questions as you want to. I want your opinions about what I say—your true opinions. Do you understand all that, Christopher Hugh?"

"Yes, Mama," he answered. "You want us to tell it like it is, right?"

"That's exactly right."

Mark was more anxious than ever for Mama to get on with it.

Bending over the shiny table and lowering her voice to a near whisper, she said, "What I'm going to tell you didn't happen today or yesterday. It happened a few weeks ago. I wanted to wait until I felt the time was right for me to tell you what I'm going to tell you.

"You both know that I've been working for Mr. Jacobs for about four months now and that I've known him awhile even before I started working for him. Well, a few weeks ago, Mr. Jacobs and I were having a conversation, when right out of the blue he asked me if I'd consider getting remarried—to him."

"Remarried!" Mark loudly exclaimed.

"Be quiet!" Mama said, quickly looking around to see if anyone might have heard him. "I don't want everyone here in the Burger Barn to hear what we're discussing. You never know who's listening."

"I can't believe it, Mama," Mark said. "I just

can't believe it. You're going to *marry* Mr. Jacobs?"

"I didn't say I was *going* to marry him. I only said he asked me if I'd consider . . ."

"Will he be our father?" Chris interrupted, looking as surprised as Mark was. "Where will he live? Why does he want to marry you?"

"I can't believe it!" Mark repeated. "I just can't believe it!"

"Is that all you can sit there and say, Mark Charles? You've said that four times already. I heard it the first time."

"I don't want him for a father," Chris said. "I don't want any more fathers. I don't even remember too much about my real father. Why would I want a fake one?"

"You were too young to remember him," she said. "But I told you many times what a good man your daddy was. I told you all the nice things I could remember about him."

"If he was so nice, why did he leave us and never come back?" Chris asked.

"This is not the time or place to talk about that now, you hear? I want you to settle down a minute. My word! I expected you both to be surprised and ask questions, but I never thought the two of you would get so crazy. I said we would talk about it, didn't I? I didn't say any decision was made. I only wanted to tell you about it."

"Yuck!" Chris exclaimed. "Why would you

20

want to marry him? I don't even know his first name. You always call him Mr. Jacobs. Do you know his first name, Mama?"

"Of course I know his first name. What does his first name have to do with anything? You call people who are older than you by their last names. That's respect. His first name is Jeremiah."

"Jere– what?" Chris asked.

"Jeremiah," she repeated.

"His mother must have hated him, giving him a name like that."

"*This* Mama is getting a little angry right now with you, Christopher Hugh. I don't want to hear one more word coming out of that tiny mouth of yours until you think about what you're going to say. Jeremiah is a fine name. It's a Bible name—like yours and Mark Charles'. Mark and Christopher are the names of saints. Saints in the Bible. Jeremiah is a Bible name, too. Jeremiah was a prophet. That's not the same as a saint, but it's close.

"Don't ever say anything like that again about anyone's mama, you hear? All mamas have good reasons for naming their children the names they best see fit. You don't know anything about Mr. Jacobs' mama."

Chris wanted to say that he didn't know anything about Mr. Jacobs either. But he could see that she was angry, that he shouldn't say another word. He almost felt like crying. But he wouldn't. He just sat, staring at Mark, biting his teeth together tightly.

Mark sat in a total state of shock. A million and one things were racing through his head.

"Do you have something to say now, Mark Charles?" she asked. "I would like to hear what you have to say."

"I can't believe it!" he repeated.

"Is that all you can sit there and say? If you say that one more time, I'm going to faint and they'll have to carry me out of this Burger Barn on a stretcher!"

"I have a lot of things to say, Mama, but I never expected anything like this. I've got to have time to think about it."

"We all have to think about it. And that's exactly what we'll do. This is just an opportunity, that's all it is. An opportunity isn't something that is definite. It's only something to think about. I didn't think you'd both react like this. Reactions come quickly—long before thoughts are thought out! At this point I don't even know what I think about it.

"One thing I do want you both to think about—all the time—is how much I love you both. I'd never do anything that would make you unhappy. Nothing! You both know that. We're a team. Now let's clean up these wrappings and go home," she said, quickly gathering the mass of paper and plastic. "No more talk now. Just thoughts."

22

Thoughts! Mark's thoughts were running faster through his head than a marathon racer could ever hope to run. Right now, if "thoughts" were a category in the Olympic Games, he would win a Gold Medal without getting up from the table! He couldn't stop thinking.

"Come along now. Let's get the chocolate-chip cookies before Mrs. Kowalski closes. We'll pick up an extra one for Mrs. Rand, too."

"She likes raisin cookies better," Chris quietly said.

"We'll get her a raisin cookie then. Mark Charles, Christopher Hugh, I love you more than anything in this world. You're my whole life. Remember to think about that."

"I love you, too, Mama," Chris said, still trying to fight back tears.

Mark didn't say anything. All he could say—to himself—was "I can't believe it!"

3

"I wouldn't do anything to upset my boys."

"Chris!" Mark called. "It's time to get up."

"I know," he answered.

"You awake? Already?"

"I didn't sleep too well last night. Mark, did Mama say anything more about Mr. Jacobs after I went to bed?" he asked, sitting up in bed, rubbing his eyes.

"No, nothing. You know how Mama is when she doesn't want to talk. She talked about everything except Mr. Jacobs. But she left a note. Just a minute and I'll get it," he said. "It's in the kitchen."

Quickly returning, he sat on the edge of Chris's bed. "It says:

24

Dear Boys:

I'll be home at the regular time—6:15. Mark Charles, put up the potatoes at about 6:00 o'clock so they'll be done in time for supper. Remember they're *new* potatoes, so you don't have to peel them. I left the raisin bran on the table. Make sure Christopher Hugh eats a *full* bowl before he goes to Wonderland.

Your lunch is on the top shelf of the fridge. Next to it is a snack for Christopher Hugh. Both of you be good in school today. And don't forget your milk money, Mark Charles. I left it . . ."

"Boy, it's a long note today, isn't it?" Chris interrupted. "But she didn't say anything about last night."

"Just a minute. There's a P.S.," Mark said, and continued reading where he had left off. " 'I left it under the note . . .' "

"You left the P.S. in the kitchen?" Chris asked.

"No, silly. The milk money was under the note. The P.S. says:

P.S. I want to think more about what I told you both last night. I wouldn't do anything to upset my boys. I want you to put it out of your minds for now. We'll talk about it tonight over supper.

I love you both very, very much.
Hugs and kisses,

Mama."

"I hate it when Mama puts things off," Chris said, "especially something like this. Do you really think she'll talk about it over supper?"

"I don't know," Mark answered. "I never really know what she's going to do next. I never expected anything like this."

"Would Mr. Jacobs live with us if they got married?" Chris asked.

"Of course he would."

"I'd rather die than have him marry Mama. He's too old. Why would she want to marry him? Why would she want to get married at all? Isn't she happy with us?" Chris asked.

"Don't get overexcited. Nothing's final yet. Mama said she wouldn't do anything to upset us."

"I'm already upset. I could hardly sleep at all last night thinking about it," Chris said.

"Well, don't show it to Mama tonight," Mark said. "Do me two big favors. If she does talk to us tonight, don't ask so many questions. Let her talk. And don't say anything about this to anyone, not even Mrs. Rand."

"Mama didn't say not to say anything."

"I know she didn't, but I don't think she would like it if we did. Let's keep this between ourselves until we really know what's going to happen."

"O.K.," Chris agreed, "but it won't be easy."

"It will be if you don't think about it. Now get ready for school or we're both going to be late. Your bus will be here soon and you're not even out of bed yet. Do what Mama said, put it out of your mind. Promise?"

"I'll try," he answered, "but that's all that's in my mind."

Mark wanted to tell him that he was upset too, but he knew it wouldn't help any. Besides, he had to put it out of his mind. Today was the day he was going to interview Mr. Carlisle for the school newspaper, something he really looked forward to.

The feature, "Meet Our School Helpers," only appeared twice a year, and it was something of an honor to get to do an interview and write it up for the school paper. His list of questions had been chosen by Dr. Chrystal, the school psychiatrist, who was also the newspaper's advisor. Mark's list had been picked from among those of six other students who competed for the assignment.

He waited outside the apartment house until the bus from Wonderland came to pick Chris up. As the bus came into sight, he said, "I'll be home a little later today. I have to do something after school. I'll pick you up at Mrs. Rand's about four fifteen."

"O.K.," Chris quietly muttered.

"Come on, Chris. Don't sound so down. Everything will work out with Mama," he said, not truly believing that it would. "You'll have time to beat Mrs. Rand at a few extra games of Old Maid this afternoon. Won't that be fun?"

"I guess so," Chris answered.

The bus pulled up. Mrs. McIntosh, the driver, opened the door with a big smile. "It's spring!" she called. "Hop in like a bunny."

Chris felt more like crawling than hopping. He wished he could have stayed home today instead of going to school. He waved to Mark as the bus pulled away.

Mark stood for a few seconds, sighed a long sigh, and started for school.

At the moment the clock hit two forty-five, Mark raised his hand.

"Can I leave now, Mrs. Cochrane?" he asked.

"Where ya' goin'?" Teddy called out loudly.

"Teddy!" Mrs. Cochrane said, in a pleasant but stern voice. "Please don't call out like that. Mark is going to do an interview with Mr. Carlisle for the school newspaper."

"So why is he goin' now? School isn't over until three fifteen. Is he special or somethin'?"

Teddy was a big pain. He was the only one in the class who gave Mrs. Cochrane a rough time. He hated school and made sure she knew it. Most of the time both the class and Mrs. Cochrane just ignored him. Mrs. Cochrane was one of the nicest, friendliest, and best teachers in the school. None of the boys and girls in the class could understand why he acted so fresh to her.

"Mark is on the school newspaper staff," she explained. "The newspaper staff is allowed time once a week to do special assignments. Mark was chosen to interview Mr. Carlisle for the next issue."

Mark wondered why she always explained things to Teddy, how she was so patient. He wished Mrs. Cochrane could give him one of Mama's looks. One of her looks when she was angry would be enough to quiet Teddy down for a month!

"Who wants to read about a school janitor?" Teddy blurted out.

This time she did ignore him. "Do you have your list of questions, Mark?" she asked.

"Yes, Mrs. Cochrane."

"And your homework assignment for tomorrow?"

"Yes, Mrs. Cochrane."

"All right, then, you can leave. Good luck with the interview, Mark." Looking directly at Teddy, she added, "We'll *all* be interested in reading your interview. Mr. Carlisle's an important person in our school. Just as important as anyone else. Good afternoon, Mark."

"Good afternoon, Mrs. Cochrane," he said,

29

leaving the classroom, walking downstairs to Mr. Carlisle's office.

"Mr. Carlisle?" he called, entering the office. "It's me, Mark Kipness. I've come to interview you."

"My goodness, is it two forty-five already? I'll be right there," Mr. Carlisle called from the boiler room.

Mark sat in the chair next to Mr. Carlisle's desk, quickly noticing how neat everything was. Papers were stacked in file folders, sharpened pencils stood in an empty marmalade jar, and a plant—a real plant, with six beautiful pinkish-white flowers—brightened the room. Mark couldn't remember ever seeing a plant that beautiful. It was much more interesting than the African violets his Great-Aunt Bertha up in Yonkers grew. And it certainly looked better than any of the plastic plants Mama had in their overcrowded apartment.

In the middle of the desk stood a small color photograph of a woman, framed in gold.

"Whew!" Mr. Carlisle exclaimed, coming into the office. "This day sped by like cars on the highway at the height of the rush hour. How are things going with you?"

"Fine," Mark answered.

"It's a great day, isn't it?"

"Yes."

"Want a carton of milk?"

"No, thank you, Mr. Carlisle. I think we should

30

begin," he said, opening his notebook and taking out a pen.

"You know, I feel a little funny being interviewed for the school paper. It's the first time anyone ever interviewed me. Custodians are always the last people to be considered important enough for something like this."

"Why do you say that?" Mark asked.

"Most people don't think my job is important," he replied.

"Yes, they do," said Mark. "Mrs. Cochrane just said you were as important as anyone else here."

"Mrs. Cochrane is a great lady. Believe me, there's a lot of responsibility in keeping a school in working order. More than most people realize. You sure you don't want some milk?"

"I'm sure," Mark answered. "I have eight questions, Mr. Carlisle. Some of the things you tell me won't be put into the paper. I only have room for four or five paragraphs."

"Four or five paragraphs, huh? I'd settle for four or five lines," Mr. Carlisle said, laughing.

Mr. Carlisle was always a pleasure to be with. He was friendly, warm, and so easy to talk to. Mark liked him a lot. Besides his many responsibilities, Mr. Carlisle found time to help the teachers and students in other ways. He had built the stage sets for the production of *The Wizard of Oz* the sixth-grade had presented last month; he helped coach the neighborhood Little League team, and even got some stores and small businesses to contribute money for Little League hats and T-shirts.

As Mark went down the list, Mr. Carlisle answered question after question. Mark took notes as fast as he could so that he wouldn't leave anything important out.

He was amazed at how much work there was in running a school. Mr. Carlisle had to know about the entire building—how the boilers operated, all about how the plumbing in the washrooms and in the hall and classroom sinks worked, how to order special supplies, and what all the safety regulations were.

The thing that impressed Mark most was his concern about keeping everything well run so that the teachers' and students' days would be free from any type of emergency.

"The last question is an easy one," said Mark. "What can the students do to help keep the school in better condition?"

"That's not as easy as it sounds, Mark," Mr. Carlisle replied. "But it is a good question. All of your questions were well thought out. Let me think about that for a second. Let's see, I think the one big thing we can all do is throw rubbish away in wastebaskets where it belongs. At the end of the day the halls really have too much litter scattered around. Candy wrappers, notebook paper, lunch bags, and sometimes even lunches that weren't eaten pop up in the strangest corners.

"If we all pitched in, a lot of my time would be saved to spend on other things. I also wish that the students, especially the younger ones, would stop trying to flush things down the toilets. They don't realize it, but they cause an awful mess. You can't imagine some of the things that get caught in the bowls. Last week alone I found two pens, a paperback book, a box of crayons, and a salami sandwich in the lower-school washroom!"

Mark didn't jot down all the items Mr. Carlisle mentioned, knowing well that he'd better stay with the litter rather than the toilet troubles. Mr. Chester, the school principal, would have a fit if the word "toilet" appeared in the school newspaper.

"Well, I guess that's it, Mr. Carlisle. Thank you very much. I certainly have a lot of work to do to put this all together."

"When will the interview appear?" asked Mr. Carlisle.

"It will be in the next issue. Oh, we'll have a picture of you, too. Wanda Lee Thompson will come to take it. She's the entire photography committee."

"If there's anything else you need, or if you want me to go over anything again, just ask. This has been fun. I'll look forward to seeing what you write about me."

"Mr. Carlisle, can I ask what that plant is? It's really pretty."

33

"That's a *Phalaenopsis*."

"Wow! That's a mouthful!" exclaimed Mark.

Mr. Carlisle laughed. "It's a name for one of the many types of orchids. They come from Asia, Africa, and Australia. I grow them as a hobby. I have a lot of them at home."

"Could you write the word down for me?" Mark asked.

"Here, take the marker," he said, pulling out a plastic strip from the clay pot and cleaning it off with a paper towel. "There's some information about it on the other side. You can bring it back to me when you're finished with it. I keep it in the pot so I know when I started raising it."

"Thanks, Mr. Carlisle. I'll return it to you tomorrow."

"Keep it as long as you need to."

"Who is the lady?" Mark asked, pointing to the photograph in the gold frame.

"My wife, Emma," Mr. Carlisle said softly, glancing at the photograph.

"Thanks again, Mr. Carlisle."

"Thank you. Have a good night, Mark."

"You, too," said Mark.

As soon as the door closed, "good night" rang through his head. He looked at his watch. It was already three forty-five. It was hard to believe he had spent a full hour with Mr. Carlisle. He had become so involved with the interview that he hadn't thought about tonight. He wanted

34

to get home quickly to find out how Chris was. Three forty-five! In just about two and a half hours Mama would be home. Six fifteen and Mama couldn't come fast enough.

4

"The new potatoes probably got older."

"Who's there?" Mrs. Rand called.

"It's me," Mark answered.

"Who?"

"It's me, Mark."

"My, that's the quietest 'It's me' I've heard in a long, long time. Come on in. Chris is in the livin' room watchin' the television set. He's been sulkin' on and off all of this afternoon. I know 'cause he only wanted to play one game of Old Maid with me. Unusual for him. Want some milk? Have some milk and half of the raisin cookie your mama sent up to me, bless her sweet heart. I saved half of it for Chris, but he didn't want it. His refusin' a raisin cookie, even half

36

of one, gives me a clue that somethin's not right."

Hearing their conversation, Chris walked into the kitchen. "Hi," he said to Mark. "We going downstairs now?"

"Yes," Mark answered. "Do you have your Old Maid?"

"Yes, let's go."

"What's the rush today?" Mrs. Rand asked. "I've a feelin' somethin's bein' a bother to both of you. If somethin' is bein' a bother, you know, you can talk to me about it. You can talk to me about anythin'."

"It's really nothing, Mrs. Rand. It's just a little late. I had to do something after school and I have some homework for tomorrow. I also have to start supper before Mama comes home."

Mark knew he could talk with her about anything. He knew how trustworthy she was. She had helped him several times before by listening and talking with him.

But he didn't want to bring up the subject of Mama and Mr. Jacobs. Not now. Besides, he had told Chris not to say anything about it. If something was going to happen, he knew he could talk to her about it then. Mrs. Rand was always there.

"You ready, Chris?" he asked.

"Yes," Chris answered. " 'Bye, Mrs. Rand. See you tomorrow."

" 'Bye, Mrs. Rand," Mark said.

"I'll see you both tomorrow, God willin'. You be sure to thank your Mama for thinkin' about me with the raisin cookie. I'll have the half I saved for dessert tonight, bein' I can't convince either of you to have it. That woman is as good as gold. In all my years on this earth I've never met a woman so wonderful and thoughtful. She's just as good as gold—even better."

Walking down the flight of stairs to their apartment, Mark asked, "You didn't say anything to her did you? About Mama?"

"No, I didn't say anything. I thought about saying something, but you told me not to."

"That's good, Chris. It's really better not to talk about it until we find out more."

"She's not dumb, you know. She knew something was wrong as soon as I came home from Wonderland. A couple of times she tried to pump me, but I didn't say anything, really I didn't."

"I believe you," Mark said, unlocking and opening the door.

Once inside, Chris went straight to the living room and turned on the television set.

"How was your day at school?" Mark asked, following him.

"O.K."

"Want me to play a game of Old Maid with you?" he asked, even though playing Old Maid was the last thing he wanted to do.

"No. I don't want to do anything."

Thank goodness, Mark thought. If he had to match Fancy Nancy or Fickle Frankie one more time—or at least now—he'd scream.

"All I keep thinking about is Mr. Jacobs marrying Mama. Yuck! Would we have to call him our father?"

"Look, don't ask me any more questions about that. Things will work out as they come up. So far nothing has happened. We'll both have plenty to think about after we hear what Mama says. Watch television for a while. I'll be in our room if you want me."

"O.K.," Chris said, sitting down on the floor in front of the television set, his back resting on the edge of the sofa.

Mark knew how he felt. He went over, sat beside him on the floor, and put his arm around his shoulder. "Aw, come on. Everything's going to be fine. I promise you that," he said.

"I hope so," Chris said. "I really hope so."

"Chris? Want to set the table?" Mark called. "It's five to six. Mama will be home in a few minutes."

Chris came into the kitchen to gather the plates, silverware, glasses, and paper napkins. Mark got the water ready for the potatoes. He was glad they were new potatoes so he didn't have to peel them.

"What's for supper?" Chris asked.

"Leftover roast beef. Mama's making hot roast

beef sandwiches with real gravy. Your favorite."

"Good," he replied. "I love Mama's gravy. It's better than that slop in the can she heats up when she's too tired to make the real stuff."

When he finished setting the table, he went back to the living room. Mark sat down to look over his notes from the interview with Mr. Carlisle. He was surprised he had taken so many notes.

When he looked up at the kitchen clock, it was six twenty-five. He closed his notebook, turned the potatoes down and went into the living room.

"Mama's late," he said. "She should be here any minute. Anything interesting on the news?"

"No," Chris answered, "same old crap."

"You'd better not let Mama hear you use that word," said Mark, surprised that Chris had said it. "She'll give you such a speech about good and bad words that you'll wish you'd never said it."

"I'm getting hungry," Chris said, ignoring Mark's warning. "Where's Mama?"

"I don't know. She's really late. She said she'd be home at six fifteen. She should be here by now."

After another five minutes passed, Mark told Chris, "I'm going to run upstairs to ask Mrs. Rand if Mama called today. Maybe she told her she'd be late and she forgot to mention it. I'll be right back."

When he came downstairs, Chris asked, "Did Mama call?"

"Yes, she called her this afternoon before you came home. But she didn't say anything about coming home late. It's twenty to seven. I'm going to call the laundry."

He dialed the number. It rang ten times but there was no answer. He hung up and dialed Mr. Jacobs' apartment, thinking that maybe Mama was with him. There was no answer there either.

"It's just not like Mama to be this late," he said. "If she was going to be this late, she would have called home and told us. I'm going to run upstairs again and ask Mrs. Rand to come down for a few minutes. Then I'm going to look for Mama. She usually takes the short way home."

"Do you think something's wrong?" Chris asked.

"No!" Mark exclaimed. "She might have stopped off at the bakery or at George's Grocery Store. I won't be long. I'm going to turn the potatoes off and get going."

"O.K.," Chris answered, "but why can't I come with you?"

"I'd rather go alone. Besides, if we both went and we missed her and she got home before us, she'd think there was something wrong. I'll be right back. Stay by the door so you can let Mrs. Rand in when she comes down," he said, nearly flying out of the apartment.

41

As he ran to the laundry, he looked on both sides of the street for Mama. He passed Mrs. Kowalski's Bake Shop and looked in the window. Mama wasn't there. He ran to the laundry, which was closed, and then on to George's Grocery Store. He looked in the window but could see she wasn't there either.

Maybe Mama did walk the longer way tonight, he thought. Maybe I missed her.

Running back, he again looked into Mrs. Kowalski's Bake Shop window. No Mama!

When he returned to the apartment building, he saw a police car pull away. Ordinarily he wouldn't have thought anything about seeing a police car in front of the building. But almost as if he had stepped into freezing water up to his waist, chills ran through him. He rushed upstairs and knocked at his door.

Mrs. Rand answered, saying, "It's just terrible. Terrible!"

"What's terrible?" he asked.

Dashing into the kitchen, he saw Mama sitting at the table. She had the strangest look on her face that he had ever seen in his entire life. Her hair was disheveled; her lipstick was smeared all under her lower lip.

"What happened, Mama?" he asked, out of breath from running.

"Your mama was mugged!" she exclaimed. "Mugged!"

"Mugged? Are you all right?" Mark asked.

"I'm fine now, but oh, did I ever get the day-lights scared right out of my skin. It was all so fast. Fast and furious."

"Terrible. Just terrible," Mrs. Rand repeated, throwing her hands into the air. "It's not safe to go out anywhere anymore. Terrible!"

"What happened, Mama?" Mark asked, totally confused.

"I just told you son. Your mama was mugged!"

"But *how* did it happen?"

"I closed the laundry at six o'clock right on the dot. Mr. Jacobs had to visit his sister, so he left the store early. I locked the lock and began walking home, thinking what a beautiful spring day this was and how much you both were going to enjoy my real gravy tonight. All of a sudden out from nowhere, some boy, a big one, a teen-ager, pushed and threw me into a doorway and tried to grab my pocketbook.

"At first I didn't even know what was happening. When I came to my senses and realized he was tugging at my pocketbook, I knew that this was it. I was being mugged! I opened my mouth and screamed so loud it scared him out of his wits. That boy must have jumped a foot before taking off."

"You're just not safe anywhere," Mrs. Rand said. "Not even in your own neighborhood."

"Did he hurt you, Mama?" Mark asked.

"No, he just shocked me to pieces. I've never been so shocked before. But I hurt him. I reached in my jacket pocket, pulled out a roll of quarters, and gave him a good knock on the back of his head. He'll have a lump that he won't forget too quickly. A roll of quarters is heavy. It might have saved my life. When I screamed, some woman, bless her soul, waved down a police car. I only wish it had been around a few minutes earlier. If it had, they might have caught that crazy while I was being mugged."

"He's probably right out there on the streets, right this very minute, waitin' to mug some other innocent woman," Mrs. Rand said.

"Officer Jason was on patrol," Mama continued, "and asked me to go down to the station to file a complaint. I didn't want to. I just wanted to get home. I had to answer a lot of questions and fill out a lot of forms. It won't do any good anyway. I was so scared that I couldn't even begin to imagine what he looked like. Just that he was young—and big. When I was through, Officer Jason drove me home. I should have called, but everything went so fast I didn't think about that until we were driving back here."

"If I could find him, I'd kill him," Chris said, screwing up his face. "Nobody's going to mug my Mama and get away with it."

"That's no way to talk," Mama snapped. "He already has mugged me and gotten away! You won't find him. If *I* don't know what he looked

44

like, and *I* was the one who was mugged, how would you find him?"

"I'd look for a mugger with a big lump on the back of his head. That's what I'd do. A big teenager with a big lump."

"You'll do nothing, you hear? Including talking like this. My mugging happened and now it's over. I was lucky that nothing serious did happen."

"Are you sure you're O.K.? Can I get you something?" Mark asked.

"No, I'm fine. I'm just a little shook up over all this excitement. This is the first time I've ever been mugged, you know. It's not a very pleasant thing."

"Pray to the good Lord above that it won't happen again," Mrs. Rand said.

"It won't happen again, not to me anyway. Muggers don't mug the same people twice. They're smarter than that. He'll just go out and try it on someone else. Sooner or later he'll get caught. Justice always wins out in the end."

"I'm beginnin' to think there isn't any justice anymore," Mrs. Rand said. "When they do catch them, what do they do? Slap them on the wrist and send them back out on the streets to terrorize more good people. There certainly isn't any justice when a woman—one as good as you—gets mugged. I don't believe there's any justice at all."

"Well, talking about it isn't going to help. It

45

happened and it's over. Let's just thank God I'm all right. I could have been knifed or something."

"I could kill him," Chris repeated.

"Christopher Hugh, I don't want to hear that come off your tongue again. Do you hear? Not now or ever. Mama doesn't like it at all. Now I think it's time we had our supper. The new potatoes probably got older by now sitting in that pot."

No one said anything.

"I don't think anyone heard what I just said. I just made a joke. Get it? The new potatoes probably got older. Isn't that funny?"

No one seemed to think so except Mama.

"Mrs. Rand," she asked, "would you like to have supper with us?"

"No, thank you, Trudy. I was halfway through a bacon, lettuce, and tomato sandwich when Mark came up. I'll finish that. You and the boys can have a quiet supper together. You could use some quiet after all this."

"You're welcome to stay, you know," Mama said. "You're always welcome in our house."

"I know, but not tonight. I'll take a rain check though. If you need me for anythin', just send Mark or Chris upstairs."

"Thank you, Mrs. Rand, but everything is fine. I'm really all right—except for the shock of it all. I never thought I'd be mugged at six o'clock at night. I never thought I'd ever be mugged at all!"

"Terrible, just terrible," Mrs. Rand said again. "I'll see you tomorrow, boys, God willin'."

"Good night, Mrs. Rand," Mark said.

"Night, Mrs. Rand," Chris added.

"Good night, darling. I'll talk to you tomorrow," Mama said.

"If not sooner," Mrs. Rand replied. " 'Bye, all."

5

"And say a little prayer . . ."

"Just look at the time," Mama said, looking at the kitchen clock. "It's already eight o'clock and we're just finishing our dessert. I'm sorry, boys, that I didn't make my real gravy tonight as I promised."

"That's O.K., Mama," Mark said.

"The canned stuff wasn't too bad," Chris added, "but it wasn't as good as yours, Mama. You make the greatest gravy in the world."

"When you promise something, you should keep it. It's important to keep promises. Remember that. Keeping promises shows you are reliable. I'll make my real gravy tomorrow night. We'll have it over mashed potatoes."

48

"Yummy!" Chris exclaimed.

"After dinner, I want to make a few phone calls," she said.

"You going to call Great-Aunt Bertha up in Yonkers?" Chris asked.

"Why would I want to call her? I spoke to her a few weeks ago."

"Don't you want to tell her you were mugged?" he asked.

"She's the last person I would call about that. It would give her something to talk about for the rest of her life. For the rest of her life she'd yack and yack about the danger of city living. She doesn't have to know about this. The whole world doesn't have to know I was mugged, especially your Great-Aunt Bertha. I want to call Dotty Schmidt."

"Is she still working at the five-and-ten-cent store?" Mark asked.

"Yes, Dotty's still there, still selling candy. I haven't seen her since I quit after Christmas. But we talk now and then on the phone. It's amazing how time flies by. We've been trying to get together for lunch for months now, but something always seems to come up. The last time we made a date, Dotty had to cancel it because her poor father had a diabetes attack. I told her I'd try to get her in tonight."

"We'll do the dishes, Mama," Mark said. "You can call her while we clean up."

"Thank you, that's nice of you to offer, but

it isn't necessary. Dotty works late tonight. The five-and-ten-cent store is open until nine o'clock on Wednesdays. Remember how late I used to come home from that job? The hours were terrible compared to the laundry. I'm glad I quit that place. It gives us more time to be together."

"Me, too," said Chris.

"I'm glad, too," Mark said.

"I won't be able to get Dotty in until nine thirty or ten. After I call her, I want to call Mr. Jacobs. He should be back from his sister's place by then. I want to let him know what happened."

Mr. Jacobs! In the midst of all the confusion, Mark and Chris had forgotten all about him. As soon as she said his name, they looked at one another. Knowing what was in Chris' mind, Mark vigorously shook his head side to side, saying without a word that this was no time to bring that matter up.

Chris received the silent message, and knew better than to say anything now. He knew Mama was upset from the mugging incident.

"I'm glad you hit that mugger with the roll of quarters," Chris said. "Maybe that will teach him a lesson."

"I think we've talked enough about that now. Besides, I'm neither proud nor pleased that I hit him. I hate violence in any way, shape, or form. It wasn't a good reaction. I wasn't thinking clearly. Fear took over my mind.

50

"We've talked about this so much that we never got the chance to talk about either of your days. What did you do at Wonderland today, Christopher Hugh?"

"Not much, Mama. Things went a little slow today. All we did was clean up the room."

"That's all right, son. Things have to go slow once in a while. We all have our slow days. They make you appreciate the fast days more. What about you, Mark Charles?"

"I had a good day, Mama. I did the interview for the school paper with Mr. Carlisle."

"Oh, my goodness! Today was the day. I forgot all about it due to my incident. How did it go?"

"It went very well. He's really a great guy. I took lots of notes. I think I'll be able to do a good article about him."

"Think? I *know* you'll do a fine job. Your writing is good. You take after my side of the family with that. I told you about my Uncle Percy, may he rest in peace. Remember my telling you that my Uncle Percy wrote a column—a *feature* column—once a week for his hometown newspaper?"

"I remember, Mama," Mark answered, smiling.

Uncle Percy wrote the obituary column for the *Pittsburgh Crier*!

"You both take after my side of the family. You're both going to grow up and be somebodies in life—somebodies special. Mama is going to see to that. When will your piece be published?"

"In the next issue. It doesn't come out though for another month. I have plenty of time to write it."

"Do it soon, while it's still fresh in your mind. Before you hand it in, I'd like to read it. I'm very interested in everything you do at school. Always try to do things while they're still fresh. While it's still fresh in my mind, perhaps we better talk about what we discussed at the Burger Barn last night."

"About you and Mr. Jacobs?" Chris blurted out, near dropping his spoon from his dish of fruit cocktail.

"Isn't that what I took you out to talk about?"

"Yes, but . . ."

"Chris!" Mark interrupted, hardly believing she would bring the subject up on her own, and not wanting her to go off onto something else.

"I could tell from your instant reactions that you weren't happy about what I told you. But I still can't understand why you both got so hot-headed, so fast. As soon as I told you about it, I knew I had made a big mistake. I could see how it disturbed you. Sometimes life takes a funny twist and there you are, confronted with something you had no idea you'd be confronted with.

"Anyway, I talked to Mr. Jacobs this afternoon and told him the idea was out of the question.

The time just isn't right to consider my getting married again. So that's final!"

"Yippee!" Chris shouted. "Am I glad. I don't like him anyway."

"That's not a nice thing to say, Christopher Hugh. You don't know him that well. He's a very kind man—kind and respectable. Sometimes people you don't think you like at first turn out to be the ones you like best. You have to have an attitude in life that everyone you meet at first is fine—until they prove themselves they're not. Now finish your fruit cocktail and we'll clean up this table. It's late. Let's get ready for the little bit of night that's left. This was a crazy day. I still can't believe I was mugged!"

"Is Chris asleep?" Mama asked, coming into the living room after finishing her call to Mr. Jacobs.

"Sound asleep," Mark answered.

"Turn down the T.V. so it won't wake him."

"It's not too loud, Mama. Besides, he's snoring louder than the T.V. volume. What did Mr. Jacobs have to say?"

"What could he say? He couldn't believe it. There isn't much to say about it. It's become a way of life these days. You just have to pray it won't ever happen to you, and if it does, like it did, you hope it'll never happen again."

"Mama, can I ask you a question?"

"You sure can, son, but why do you ask if you can ask? Why don't you just ask what you want to ask?"

"Because I know you're tired out, Mama."

"I'm never too tired to talk to you. What is it?"

"Do you love Mr. Jacobs?"

"I don't love him, Mark Charles. I respect him. People can respect and be kind to one another without loving them. Love takes a long time to grow between people. You grow into love."

"Was Mr. Jacobs mad or anything when you told him you didn't want to get married?"

"No, he's not the type to get mad. I think he knew the answer all along. I think I knew the answer right from the start, too. Now that I look back on it, I can understand Christopher Hugh's and your reactions. I've been doing a lot of thinking about it. Although Mr. Jacobs is a good man, he really isn't the one I'd like to live with for the rest of my life. Choosing a partner is a tough decision to make. Choosing a partner for all three of us is an even harder decision.

"I did want to tell you and your little brother about it, though, just to get your thoughts. Mr. Jacobs respects me very much. I think he was a little disappointed, but he'll get over that. He's really a fine person."

"Is this the first time anyone asked you to get married since Dad left?"

"Yes, it is. And you know, son, it felt funny.

54

Funny and kind of nice at the same time. It's good to know someone really cares about you so much that they'd ask you to consider marrying them."

"Have you ever thought about getting married again?"

"Once in a while it does come into my mind. I don't think I'd like to go through life being alone forever. I'd like to have a companionship with a man some day. If the right one—the right man for the three of us—came along, I think I would remarry. That's if you both approved. But that's not going to happen for a long time to come. It would take a very special man to want to marry someone with two growing boys."

"Did you love Dad?" he asked.

She was silent for minute before answering.

"Yes, of course I loved him. We loved one another very much. Our love brought both of you into the world. That's more love than many people know in a lifetime. But just as love can grow, it can die, too. Your daddy's love for us died because he was troubled by the times. He couldn't take the pressures of struggling day to day. He never managed to get a break. He was stuck in factory jobs year after year that never paid much. He never had a chance to better himself. I guess he just got fed up with everything and wanted out from any responsibility."

"Do you ever miss him, Mama?"

"Do you?" she asked.

"Sometimes I do," Mark answered. "Sometimes I think it would be fun to have Dad around."

"That's natural, son. There are times I wish he was around here, too. At first I missed him terribly. But that turned to anger and finally to forgiveness. I knew the minute I signed the divorce papers that we'd never see him again. I'll never understand, though, how a man like your daddy could walk out on me and you two fine boys and not get in touch with us again. Sometimes I do miss not having a husband to love and share things with."

"You have us, Mama, all the time."

"I'm thankful for that, son. You and your little brother are my whole life. But there are different kinds of love. The love between a mother and her children is different from the love a man and woman share. When you get older you'll understand that. Mama has a lot of love in her heart. Being loved and loving somebody back is still the most important ingredient in life."

Mark didn't say any more. He could sense her loneliness. Even though she didn't think so, he was old enough to understand her feelings. He understood more than she could ever imagine.

They sat quietly watching the news together. When it was over, she said, "I'm going to bed now. You should too. This night flew by, didn't it?"

"It sure did," Mark answered.

"In your prayers tonight, son, thank God for not causing me to have any physical harm today. And say a little prayer for that boy who mugged me, too."

"What?"Mark asked, startled."Why should I pray for him?"

"Because he probably can't help what he did. Maybe a prayer or two will help. You never know. The Bible says that God works in mysterious ways. He certainly worked funny today, but He must have had His good reason. Good night, son," she said, kissing him on the cheek. "I love you. Sleep tight and don't let the bedbugs bite."

"Night, Mama. I love you, too. I'll see you tomorrow."

"I'll leave a note for you on the kitchen table."

"Good. Chris and I love your morning notes. Sleep well, Mama."

He turned off the television set and went to his bedroom. It had been a wild day!

6

"This world has really turned upside down."

Mark had worked hard the past week writing the interview with Mr. Carlisle. He was anxious to hear what Dr. Chrystal would say about it.

Entering his office, he immediately noticed how different it was from Mr. Carlisle's. Papers were scattered all over the desk, books were piled high on the floor, and the small room reeked of stale cigar smoke.

Dr. Chrystal was on the telephone. "Yes, yes, fine," he was saying. "Fine. Good. Wednesday afternoon at three will be fine. Good-bye now."

Banging down the receiver, he turned to Mark and said, "Phones! Half of my life is spent on the phone. Now what are you here for?" he asked.

"The interview," Mark answered, "with Mr. Carlisle."

"Oh, yes, the interview. Now let's see, I have it here somewhere," he said, scrambling through a mass of papers. "Ah, here it is. There's only a few things I want changed."

Skimming the interview, he stopped, saying, "Take out the phrase about Mr. Carlisle's *Phalae*- whatever it is."

"It's an interesting word," Mark said. "It's the name of a type of orchid. I explain that in the next sentence."

"I know you explain it. I can read," he said, somewhat annoyed, "but no one else will be able to read it. Besides, economy of words is important in newspaper writing. Let's just say he grows orchids as a hobby," he added, crossing out the sentences with a red pencil.

Mark was becoming quite uneasy. He hoped he wouldn't change too much more.

"Now let's see, there's one other thing here at the end. Here it is—about his wife, Emma. Didn't he tell you that his wife is dead?"

"Dead!" Mark said, surprised. "No, he didn't. I noticed the photograph on his desk and asked him about it. He just told me it was his wife. I never thought . . ."

"When you're doing an interview you've got

to think," Dr. Chrystal interrupted. "Do you know how embarrassing it would be for him, and you—and me—if something like this appeared in the school newspaper? We'll just cut it out and end with his quote about all of us pitching in to keep the school clean."

"I'm really sorry I didn't ask him more about his wife," Mark said, feeling stupid that he hadn't.

"That's what I'm here for—to check out all the facts."

"When did his wife die, Dr. Chrystal?"

"A few years ago. Before he came here. Mr. Carlisle lives alone. He has an apartment in the same building as I do. He's by himself, like me."

"Do you want me to write the interview over?" Mark asked. "I can do it over the weekend and have it back on Monday."

"No, that isn't necessary. Mrs. Potter, the school aide, will type it up on Monday or Tuesday. You did a good job on this, Mark, except for the one mistake—the one *big* mistake. There's no room for mistakes in newspaper writing. You keep that in mind for the future.

"Before you go, can you tell me a good time when your mother can come in to see me next week?"

"What for?" Mark asked.

"I'm having parent interviews about the tests your class took last month. It's a new rule set down by the P.T.A. that every parent, or at least one of them in each family, is seen to discuss the results. Fathers are impossible to get. It's easier to get mothers to come in."

"My mother works, Dr. Chrystal, but she does have Mondays off. Do you want me to tell her to call you?"

"No, all that calling back and forth is just a waste of time. Give me her number at work and I'll call her a little later. Maybe she can come in on Monday. I want to get this over with as soon as I can."

Mark gave him the telephone number at the laundry and told him he could reach her before six o'clock. But he couldn't understand why Mama had to come in to see him.

"Mrs. Cochrane said I did very well on the test," he said. "Monday is my mama's only day off, and she has a lot of things to do. Couldn't I just tell her I did very well?"

"No!" Dr. Chrystal snapped. "I have a lot of things to do too, you know. Whether you came in number one or last on the list, I have to see one of your parents. There are rules I have to follow. If your mother is so busy, how about your father?"

"My parents are divorced, Dr. Chrystal. It'll have to be my mama who comes in to see you."

"Everyone's divorced these days. I'll call your mother a little later. I have to finish up a million and one things before I leave here today. Besides my *real* work, I have this blasted newspaper to do. There's no end. You can leave now," he said abruptly.

"Thanks," Mark said, glad that the meeting was over.

Dr. Chrystal didn't answer. He was mumbling something about test scores and parents while dialing another telephone number.

"Trudy, it's for you," Mr. Jacobs called, resting the telephone receiver on the counter.

"Be right there," she called back. "Who is it?"

"Mrs. MacLaughlin from P.S. six eighty-six."

"Oh, my goodness!" she exclaimed, dropping the laundry basket and running to the phone. "What is she doing calling me this late on a Friday afternoon? I hope nothing's wrong.

"Rosie?" she asked, picking up the receiver. "What's up?"

"Nothing's ever up here," Rosie answered. "You should've asked 'What's down?' and I could give you a list as long as your arm. How've you been, Trudy?"

"Fine, just fine."

"I heard you were attacked on the street," Rosie said. "It's awful. You're not safe to walk anymore, even in broad daylight."

"That's all over with now, Rosie. Is that why you called?"

"No, it isn't, honey, but I figured since I'm talking with you I'd just offer my sympathies. I don't know what I'd do if something like that

62

happened to me. Listen, honey, the reason I'm calling is that Mark said you were off on Mondays. Dr. Chrystal would like to make an appointment with you this coming Mon—"

"Dr. Chrystal? Who's Dr. Chrystal?" Mama interrupted.

"Chrystal's the school psychiatrist. Can you make it at about two thirty this coming Monday?"

"What is this all about?"

"Honey, he doesn't tell me what it's *about.* He only tells me to make appointments. Apparently it's about Mark. How's two thirty?"

"Two thirty is fine."

"Great. I've got you down, Trudy."

"I wish you could tell me what this is about. Why would a psychiatrist want to talk to me about Mark Charles?"

"Look, I told you he doesn't tell me anything. I'm only the school secretary. Since I work here I can't say too much. You know how it is, honey. You talk too much and it gets back to those you don't want it to get back to in the first place. Maybe Mark knows more. They tell the kids more than they tell me. Look, honey, I have to run. I'll see you on Monday at two thirty. Happy weekend, Trudy. And stay safe!"

"I will, Rosie. You have a good weekend, too."

"Anything wrong?" Mr. Jacobs asked.

"No, I don't think so. I have to go to school on Monday. It's something about Mark Charles."

"Well, I know if it's about Mark, there's nothing wrong. That's one great kid you have there."

"Boy!" Mama snapped. "He's one of *two* great *boys* I have."

"Yoo-hoo! Mama's home," she called, opening the apartment door. "Mark Charles, where are you?"

"I'm in my room. I'll be out in a second."

"Another second is too long for me to wait. Far too long," she said, immediately appearing at the doorway. "Where's Christopher Hugh?"

"He's upstairs playing Old Maid with Mrs. Rand. I'll go up and get him."

"Never mind that now. There's something I want to talk with you about. Remember my telling you, and telling you often, that honesty is the best policy? You have to be honest about things."

"Honest about what, Mama?"

"I want you to be honest about everything, especially with me."

"Is something the matter, Mama?"

"Yes, there is something the matter. The matter is that I got a call this afternoon from Rosie MacLaughlin. She wants me to come to school on Monday to meet the school psychiatrist. It has to be about you."

"I know, Mama," Mark said casually.

"You know? What do you mean you know?"

"I met with Dr. Chrystal today about the interview with Mr. Carlisle."

"What does that have to do with me?"

"Nothing, Mama. When we finished, he asked me for your number at the laundry. He wants to see you about a test I took."

"What about the test? What kind of a test was it? Is there something wrong with you? If you know something that I don't know about I want you to tell me—*now*! Are you all right?"

"I'm fine, Mama."

"Have you had any dizzy spells lately? Or headaches? Even if you had the tiniest of dizzy spells or the tiniest of headaches, I want you to tell me about them."

"Mama, nothing's wrong. Dr. Chrystal is seeing all of the fifth-grade parents about the test. He said it's a P.T.A. rule. I did very well on the test. Mrs. Cochrane told me I had one of the highest scores in both classes."

"Is that all? Are you sure that's all?" she asked.

"That's all, Mama. Really."

"I don't know why those school psychiatrists don't give you a message. That doctor didn't even tell Rosie MacLaughlin what it was about. It's basic manners for someone to leave a message, especially when it's something from a doctor-psychiatrist. Why, even when Mr. Jacobs or I have to make a call about someone's laundry, we leave a message. Basic manners is what that is.

"I had some time all afternoon worrying about you. It's the first time in my life I ever got a call to go and see a psychiatrist. You should only know the thoughts that raced through my head. I didn't even tell Mr. Jacobs it was the psychiatrist who wanted to see me. What is this doctor like?"

"He's O.K., Mama, but he always seems a little annoyed and disturbed about everything."

"The psychiatrist is disturbed? That's just what I need. To spend my afternoon off visiting a disturbed psychiatrist! What's the matter with him?"

"Nothing, really. He just seems unhappy with everything. He never even smiles. And he's frumpy."

"Frumpy? What kind of way is that to talk about someone? That isn't the kindest of words to use to describe a person—especially a doctor-psychiatrist."

"Well he is frumpy, Mama. He's frumpy-looking and he dresses frumpy. His suit is always wrinkled and his shirts and ties always have spots on them. He isn't like Mr. Carlisle. Mr. Carlisle is happy all the time. No matter how busy he is, he always has a big smile. He's sharp-looking, too."

"This world has really turned upside down. Psychiatrists are frumpy and custodians are sharp-looking. Crazy! Just crazy!"

"I made a mistake in the interview, Mama.

Dr. Chrystal didn't like it. I mentioned that Mr. Carlisle is married."

"He is, isn't he? I read the piece you did. You told me he had his wife's picture on his desk—in a gold frame. See how I remember everything you tell me? Every little detail right down to the gold frame."

"His wife is dead, Mama. He lives by himself."

"Oh, that's a terrible shame. Just terrible. May she rest in peace, the poor thing. But a mistake like that could happen to anyone. If he told you it was his wife in the gold frame and he didn't tell you she passed on, how would you know?"

"I guess I should have asked him more about her. Dr. Chrystal said it was a big mistake."

"Well, on Monday I'll let him know that people can't know everything if people they're talking with don't tell them. A psychiatrist should know that."

"Mama, please don't say anything about the interview. It's all done now. I don't even have to write it over. He only wants to talk about the test. Promise you won't say anything to him about the interview?"

"I promise. If you don't want me to, I won't. You don't know how much better I feel. I feel brand-new again. Oh, the things that went through my head. I promise I won't say a word about the interview, but I am going to tell him—in a nice way, of course—that he should have the basic manners to leave a message, especially on a Friday. This would have been a worrisome weekend for nothing if you didn't know what I was going in for. Worrisome and pointless!

"Mark Charles, did you say anything to Rosie MacLaughlin about my being mugged?"

"No, Mama. I didn't say a word to anybody. You told me not to."

"She mentioned it on the phone this afternoon. I don't know how she found out about it."

"Someone must have told her. Even Mrs. Cochrane knew," Mark said.

"Bad news travels fast in this neighborhood. You can't keep nothing from nobody. Did you get a chance to see the super about fixing that dripping kitchen faucet?"

"Yes, Mama. He said he'd try to get to it next week."

"Next week and next week. That faucet's been leaking for two weeks now. I don't know why he can't do it and get it over with. It's not only wasting precious water, it's starting to drive me nuts. I'll have to put some pressure on him. Before he gets around to it, there could be a water shortage throughout the entire country. Maybe on Sunday we'll look in Barker's Hardware for something to stop it. If Barker's doesn't have something, maybe we can find a book in the library on fixing leaky faucets. I know a lot about a lot of things, but I don't know anything about plumbing. I do know that I want it fixed, though."

"He said he'd try to fix it next week. We'd better wait for him to do it, Mama."

Mark didn't want to remind her of the time she had tried to stop the toilet from running and blocked it up for two days before a plumber could get in to fix it.

"Well, I'll try to see him about it. The problem is that he's never around when you want him. I'm going to change my clothes now. Why don't you run up and get Christopher Hugh? We'll have an early supper tonight."

"O.K., Mama. I'll be right back."

7

". . . everyone will point at me and say, 'That's his mama.'"

Dr. Chrystal went on and on talking about the final results of the test scores.

"As you can see here, Mrs. Kaplan . . ."

"Kipness," she corrected. "I'm Mrs. Kipness."

"Sorry," he said. "Mrs. Kaplan was here just before you came in."

Pointing to a computer printout, he said, "Mark came in quite high on the MAT."

"The mat?" she asked, wondering why he was tested on a mat.

"Yes, MAT," he answered. "That stands for the Mental Aptitude Test, which is part of SAT."

"Sat?" she asked.

"Yes, that stands for Scholastic Aptitude Test."

"Oh," she answered, becoming quite anxious over the barrage of words he was spilling out.

"The state law," he continued, "establishes results to include a number of percentages in proportion to the students the county will . . ."

He's a walking encyclopedia, she thought. A running encyclopedia! She clutched her pocketbook, hoping he would finish soon. He spoke in such big words that he might just as well have talked to her in Greek!

"Do you have questions, Mrs. Kipness?" he asked, after finishing another lengthy sentence.

"Just one," she answered. "Can you tell me what all this means?"

"It means that Mark has a good chance to compete in the ACT, the Aptitude College Testing program in high school, and possibly score high enough to receive a scholarship. I would assume plans are in the air for Mark to go to college."

"Of course they are," she said. "Both my boys are going to get a college education. They're going to have every opportunity I never had. I'll see to that."

"I didn't know you had another child in school," he said.

"He's not in this school. Christopher Hugh goes to the Wonderland Kindergarten Project. It's a Head Start Center for bright children. Very bright children. When I read about it in the

71

newspaper, I immediately went down to enroll him. You'll never know how hard it was for me to get him into the project. I had to fill out a million and one papers. But it was all worth it. Wonderland has done wonders for my boy. He'll be coming here next fall. Someday this school will be proud of both my boys. I wouldn't be surprised at all if years from now they named the building after them."

"The last thing I have to show you is Mark's SIT—Social Intelligence Test. If you look at this . . ."

MAT, SAT, ACT, SIT, she thought to herself. It all sounded like a class of dogs being trained at an obedience school.

As Dr. Chrystal continued, she thought about what Mark Charles had said about him—that he was frumpy. He was! He looked to her as if he had never had a hearty laugh in his entire life—not even a good smile. She felt a little sorry about that, but at the same time she was proud that Mark Charles was such a good judge of character. He had summed up Dr. Chrystal perfectly—frumpy!

"Well, that's it, Mrs. Kipness," he said. "That is, unless you have anything to ask about the test results."

She couldn't have asked anything if she had wanted to. She had no idea what he had rambled on about except that Mark Charles' scores were among the highest. And she couldn't understand why he couldn't just say that without boring her with all his million-dollar words.

"I have nothing more to ask about this," she answered.

"Good," he replied. "It was pleasant to have met you, Mrs. Kipness. It's always a pleasure to meet the mother of a student who's as fine as your Mark."

"Thank you," she said, getting up from the chair. "My word! It's five past three already. I'm meeting Mark Charles downstairs. We're going to do some food shopping together."

"Again, thank you for coming in. If you have any questions later on, don't hesitate to call me."

"I do have one question, sir," she said, "but it's not about Mark Charles or the test."

"Yes?" he asked.

"Where do you take your shirts to be cleaned?"

The question nearly knocked him over. He was quiet for a second.

"Uh, I take them to Perkins-Perfect-Plus, the dry cleaner in the shopping center."

"Well, they're not that perfect. They don't do a good job. I work down at Mr. Jacobs' Laundry on Strand Street, right across from Dora's Delicatessen. I promise you if you bring them in to me, I'll do a better job. We're not as big as Perkins; they can't afford to give special attention to their customers the way we do. I'll have your shirts looking as good as new in just one washing. And if I don't, and you're not satisfied, Mr. Jacobs won't charge you a cent. Satisfied customers keep coming back and that's what business is all about. Come in any day except Monday. We're closed on Mondays."

"Thank you, Mrs. Kipness. I just might do that."

"You won't be sorry. Good-bye, sir," she said. "It's good to know my son is doing so well. Not that I'm surprised at that, but it's always good to hear—especially from a doctor-psychiatrist. See you at the laundry," she added, walking out of his office—gladly!

Mark was waiting at the bottom of the stair-case. As she walked down, he asked, "How did it go, Mama?"

"Fine, just fine."

"What did he say?"

"He said you did very well on the test."

"I told you that, Mama. I told you you didn't have to worry about anything. You didn't say anything to him about the interview, did you?"

"No, I didn't. You asked me not too and I said I wouldn't. I always keep my promises. Be-sides, I could hardly get a word in edgewise. He talks like an encyclopedia. Mark Charles, you know your Mama never likes to say anything bad about people, especially a doctor-psychia-trist, but you were right about him—he is frumpy!"

Mark laughed.

"Let's get going now. I want to get to Foods-for-You to pick up some of those specials. They have double coupons this week and we can save a lot of money."

"Mama, before we go, come downstairs with me. I have to return Mr. Carlisle's plant marker and I'd like you to meet him. It'll only take a few minutes."

"Fine," she said. "Lead the way, son."

Walking into his office, Mark called, "Mr. Carlisle? It's me, Mark."

"Be right there," he answered from the boiler room.

In just a few seconds he came into his office. "Hi, Mark, how's it going?" Noticing Mama, he said, "Oh, hello, ma'am. Can I help you with something?"

"I'm Mrs. Kipness," she said. "Mark Charles' mama."

"Mike Carlisle," he said, shaking her hand. "Glad to meet you."

"I'm glad to meet you, too. I feel I know you already from the fine interview Mark Charles wrote about you for the school paper."

"Won't you sit down?" he asked.

"No, thank you, sir. Mark Charles and I have some food shopping to do."

"I just wanted to return the plant marker to you, Mr. Carlisle. The one you lent me from the orchid plant."

"Mark Charles was right about that plant," she said, admiring the orchids blazing in full bloom. "It really is a beautiful sight. Amazing."

"They're quite easy to grow," Mr. Carlisle said. "No trouble at all."

"Maybe not for you," she answered. "I bet you're a man who's always had a green thumb. I've never had any luck with houseplants. None at all."

"We have a lot of plastic plants," Mark said.

"That's all I can handle," Mama added. "Plastic doesn't take any care. They look the same all the time. But naturally, they're not as pretty as this one is. If I had more time, I'd try growing something like that, but I'm a working woman."

"What do you do, Mrs. Kipness?"

"I work at Mr. Jacobs' Laundry. I'm his partner."

"Oh, that's a good business to be in."

"It sure is," she answered. "And it gets better all the time. Since I joined up with Mr. Jacobs, business has almost tripled. That's because I'm a dedicated worker. From Mark Charles' interview I could tell you were dedicated to your job, too. And that's good. So many people slough off these days that you begin to wonder how this wild world functions. Dedicated people— like you and me—are at a rare premium these days."

"You're very right, Mrs. Kipness," he said.

"Yeah, not like our apartment building super, huh, Mama?" Mark said.

"Why do you bring him up now, son? Mr. Carlisle isn't interested in our personal problems."

"What's the problem with him?" Mr. Carlisle asked Mark.

"We've had a leaky kitchen faucet for over two weeks now. Mama says if he doesn't fix it soon there will be a water shortage throughout the country."

Mr. Carlisle laughed.

"Come, now, Mark Charles. Let's not take up Mr. Carlisle's valuable time with our leaky faucet problem. I think we should go now. He has enough to do. It was good meeting you, sir."

"Mr. Carlisle, is there a good way to fix a leaky faucet? Something Mama and I can do to stop it?"

"It probably just needs a washer—a little round piece of metal that fits right under the faucet. But you have to have the right size. Look, if it's all right with you, Mrs. Kipness, I can stop by one afternoon this week and take a look at it. It can probably be fixed in a minute or two. I have a big supply of washers—one of them will do the trick."

"Why, that's quite kind of you, sir," she said, "but I wouldn't think of imposing on your time. Nor your talent."

"Time is something I have plenty of. I really

wouldn't mind it at all. I'll drop by one afternoon when Mark is home. The faucet will be fixed before you get home from your business."

"Mama, if we wait for the super to look at it, we could wait forever."

"Well, if you truly don't mind doing it, it would be fine. But I'd want to pay you for your time and trouble."

"No way," he said. "It'll be my way of paying back Mark for doing the interview with me. I am quite proud of that. Mark, just let me know when you'll be home and I'll drop by."

"If you're going to be so kind and go through all that trouble, sir, I'd like very much if you'd drop over when I'm home," she said. "That way I can watch what you're doing so I'll know what to do if it ever happens again. Why don't you have dinner with us this coming Thursday—that is if you like spaghetti and meatballs? Thursday's Italian night at our house."

"Mama makes real good sauce, Mr. Carlisle," Mark said, delighted that she had asked him to dinner. "Even better than any you get in Italian restaurants."

"That would be great, Mrs. Kipness. I do enjoy Italian food, especially homemade."

"Then we'll see you on Thursday. How's seven o'clock?"

"Great. Seven on Thursday it is."

"See you then," she said. "And thank you very much."

"Good-bye, Mr. Carlisle," Mark said.

"Good-bye, Mark. It was very nice meeting you, ma'am," Mr. Carlisle said.

"You, too, sir. 'Bye again."

"Oh, your address. I don't have the address," he said.

"That's as easy as pie," she told him. "It's the big apartment house on Elm Street—333 Elm Street, apartment number 33. Just remember three-three-three, number three-three, on the street named after the tree."

He jotted the address on a piece of notepaper. "Till Thursday," he said.

"He's quite a nice man," Mama said as they walked toward Foods-for-You. "Quite nice."

"I told you that, didn't I, Mama? I knew you'd like him. Isn't he different from Dr. Chrystal?"

"Different? There's a world of difference between them. I could tell the minute I met him. When he talks, he makes sense. That doctor uses too many big words.

"Mama, why did you tell him you were Mr. Jacobs' partner? A partner means that you own half of the business, doesn't it?"

"In a way it does, and in another way it doesn't. It slipped out. It was wrong of me to tell him that—and yet it wasn't. Since there's only Mr. Jacobs and I at the laundry—two of us—I suppose we could be considered partners. But if I gave the impression I owned half of the place, it was wrong. We should always be careful what words we choose to use. I've told you and your little brother that many times. Once specific words come off your tongue, there's no way to put them back on. If he ever asks about it again, I'll explain to him the real kind of partnership I have at the laundry. But he won't ask about it. He's only coming to fix the faucet and for spaghetti and meatballs. He's not interested in my work at the laundry."

Changing the subject, she added, "I'm proud of your test scores, son. You're one of the best students in the class. I'm proud as proud can be. Keep doing well in school. Someday you'll be somebody—somebody big—and everyone will point at me and say, 'That's his mama.' That'll be some day for me, son. Some day indeed!"

8

"You sure pick some funny times to start asking silly questions."

"I still can't believe how quickly you fixed the faucet, Mr. Carlisle," she said. "It was like magic. Wasn't it just like magic, boys?"

"Yes, Mama," Chris said. "Can I have another meatball?"

"You sure have an appetite tonight, son. This will be the third meatball you've had."

"They're delicious," he said. Looking up at the kitchen clock he announced, "It's seven forty-five."

Mr. Carlisle automatically turned around to look at the time, noticing the plastic clock shaped like a tomato.

81

"That's wonderful, son," said Mama. "Just wonderful."

"What's so wonderful about seven forty-five?" asked Mark.

Mr. Carlisle thought the same thing, but didn't say anything.

"Your little brother just told the time. That's what's wonderful. He's beginning to know all the time."

"I've been learning fifteens, thirties and forty-fives at Wonderland," said Chris, feeling quite proud.

"Hey, that is nice, Chris," Mark said. "Congratulations."

Mr. Carlisle smiled, realizing what a big moment it was for Chris.

"I already know hours. I'll let you know when it's eight fifteen next, O.K.?"

"That will be just fine," Mama said. "But now I think you should eat your spaghetti and meatballs before it gets too cool."

"Everything's really delicious, Mrs. Kipness," Mr. Carlisle said.

Chris looked up at the clock again. Quickly, he started to tug on Mama's knee, first gently, then a little harder. She kept taking his hand off.

"I think you should be eating now, Christopher Hugh." Under her breath, she added, "You're acting a little bit strange, you know. Stop it!"

He twirled his fork around in the spaghetti. Putting it to his mouth, he looked at the clock and again tugged Mama's knee. This time she slapped his hand under the table. The spaghetti fell from his fork onto his lap.

Since Mark and Mr. Carlisle were talking together, neither of them noticed.

Mama did!

Chris picked up the spaghetti with a paper napkin. Mama gave him one of her if-looks-could-kill-you looks.

All of a sudden he furiously began blinking his eyes, trying to get Mama's attention. He fluttered them up and down, opening and closing them, so fast he nearly got dizzy.

"Is there something the matter?" Mr. Carlisle asked, noticing him.

"No, everything's fine. The spaghetti's real good," Chris said. "Mama, can I leave the table for a minute, please? I forgot to do something in my room," he said, winking and blinking at her.

"You're acting a little silly, son. Mama doesn't like it when you act this silly, especially at the dinner table, and especially when we have a guest. Maybe it would be a good idea if you left the table for a minute or so. Maybe you'll come back with your senses straight."

"Excuse me," Chris said, standing up so quickly he nearly knocked over the kitchen chair. He dashed away from the table into his room. He opened his drawer, tore a piece of paper from his drawing tablet, grabbed a brown and a red crayon, and went to work, drawing as fast as he could a tomato-shaped clock with a very big brown cockroach sitting in the middle.

He folded it in half and ran through the hall. He held the drawing behind him as he walked back to the table to sit down.

Mr. Carlisle was still talking to Mark.

Chris unfolded the drawing on his lap and slipped it into Mama's.

She looked at it, then quickly looked up at the clock. As in Chris' picture, a very big brown cockroach was sitting right between the big hand and the little hand.

"Oh, my word!" she loudly exclaimed.

"What's the matter, Mama?" Mark asked.

"Oh, nothing, dear. I just remembered I have to turn off the gas burner under the spaghetti pot. You two keep on chatting," she said, getting up from the chair.

She walked over to the stove, grabbed a spatula, and knocked the clock. The cockroach scurried behind it. She prayed she had scared it enough that it would stay put before Mr. Carlisle had a chance to notice it.

Returning to the table, she said, "Mark, why don't you and Mr. Carlisle go into the living room while I begin to clear the table?"

"We didn't have dessert yet, Mama," he said.

"We'll have dessert *after* I clean up the spaghetti dishes," she told him, peering at the clock. "Go into the living room—*now!*"

Mark couldn't imagine why all of a sudden she was acting so strange. Chris was acting a little weird, too, sitting fluttering his eyes at him. He wondered if Mr. Carlisle thought anything about it.

"Christopher Hugh, finish that meatball now and help me set the table for our dessert."

Trying desperately to distract Mr. Carlisle's attention from the kitchen clock, she took his arm, moving him over to a corner where he couldn't see it.

"This is my salt-and-pepper collection," she told him. "Aren't they nice?"

Before he had a chance to say anything, she led him into the living room. Mark followed, beginning to think she was going crazy.

"You two sit right here for just a while and I'll be back in a flash. It'll only take a few seconds for me to set the table for dessert. Be right back," she said, fleeing from the living room.

"Quick!" she whispered to Chris. "Get up and get the can of roach spray."

"I tried to tell you . . ."

"Sh-h-h!" she commanded. "Whisper. I don't want Mr. Carlisle to hear."

"I tried to tell you about the cockroach," he

whispered, going to the closet at the bottom of the sink. "Why do you think I was tugging your knee?"

"I thought you might be showing off in front of Mr. Carlisle. I'm sorry," she said. "Quick, give me the roach spray."

She took the can, shook it, and lifted the clock from the wall. The cockroach began running. She ran after it.

"That roach spray will smell up the whole kitchen," Chris whispered. "It stinks. Mr. Carlisle will smell it."

"You're right," she said. "Grab that plastic cup. When the cockroach stops moving, put it over him."

"How do you know it's a him?" he asked. "It could be a her cockroach!"

"You sure pick some funny times to start asking silly questions. Just do what I say, you hear? When it crawls into the cup, put your hand over it and trap it. Then go and flush it down the toilet."

"Good idea," Chris said.

"I haven't seen a cockroach in this apartment for months. I don't know where that thing could have come from. And I don't know why it decided to move into our kitchen right at the time we have company. I'd die a thousand deaths if Mr. Carlisle saw that big thing. He'd think we'd live like pigs!"

"I got it, Mama," Chris said.

86

"Good. Get rid of it. Make sure it goes all the way down the bowl. Then wash your hands and get back out here at once. Mr. Carlisle must think I'm crazy, shuffling him away from the table like that. Hurry up!"

"I guess I should get going," Mr. Carlisle said. "I really had a lovely evening, Mrs. Kipness. Mark was right about your Italian cooking. It's the best spaghetti and meatballs I've ever had."

"That's kind of you to say, Mr. Carlisle," she said, "but I don't believe a word of it."

"It is true. It's the best."

"Well, if you say it's true, it must be. At least I like hearing it," she said, smiling.

"You should taste her brown gravy," Chris said. "Mama makes the best gravy in the whole world."

"I bet she does," Mr. Carlisle said. "Mrs. Kipness, I hope you don't think I'm being forward or anything like that, but the circus is coming to New York for a few weeks. I thought perhaps you and the boys might like to go with me."

"The circus!" Chris yelled. "Yippee! Can we go? Can we Mama?"

"Mark?" she asked.

"I'd love it," he answered. "We've never seen a real live circus before—only ones on television."

"Really?" Mr. Carlisle asked. "Well, this one is Ringling Brothers, Barnum & Bailey—the big-

87

gest circus in the world. They call it 'The Greatest Show on Earth'—and for good reason. It is the greatest. It's spectacular. I've been going every year since I was a teenager."

"Will there be a real live elephant?" Chris asked.

"There'll be dozens of them. Ringling Brothers has dozens of everything."

"It's very nice of you to ask, Mr. Carlisle. I think we'd all enjoy it very much. I haven't been to a circus myself since I was a little girl. My grandmother, may she rest in peace, used to take me when I was growing up in Pittsburgh. It wasn't like Ringling Brothers, though. It only had one ring."

"It's all set then. I'll get tickets for a Sunday afternoon performance. Consider it a date. Thanks again, Mrs. Kipness. I had a great night."

"We enjoyed having you, Mr. Carlisle," she said.

They all said good night at the door. Before leaving, Mr. Carlisle turned to her. "By the way, Mrs. Kipness, since we'll be seeing one another again soon, please call me Mike."

"Mike it is," she said, "but only if you call me Trudy."

"Good night, Trudy," he said. "Good night, boys."

Closing the door, she asked, "Did you have a good time tonight, boys?"

"The best part just happened," Chris said. "We're going to the circus! Do you think he really meant it, Mama?"

"Of course he meant it. He wouldn't have asked us if he didn't. He looks like a man of his word."

"Mama," Mark asked, "why were you and Chris acting so weird at the dinner table? And why did you send us into the living room before we had dessert?"

"There was a cockroach on the clock," Chris said. "A big one. I saw it first."

"What's the big deal about a cockroach being on the clock? I'm sure Mr. Carlisle's seen cockroaches before," Mark said.

"He may have seen them before," Mama said, "but not in *our* house. I thought I'd die when Christopher Hugh let me know about it. That was clever of you, son, to do that drawing," she added, showing Chris' picture to Mark.

"Thanks, Mama," Chris said. "It was the best thing I could think of."

"What did you do with it?" Mark asked.

"I flushed it down the toilet and drowned it," Chris answered.

"I still don't know what's so terrible about having a cockroach in the house."

"They're a sign of filth," Mama said. "Pure filth. Don't you think Mr. Carlisle's stomach might have turned if he saw a cockroach crawling around the wall while he was eating? He'd think I kept a filthy kitchen."

"It's not true, Mama," Mark said. "They're not a sign of filth. They're insects just like flies and mosquitoes. Cockroaches have been around before people—even before the dinosaurs."

"You an expert on cockroaches?" Chris asked.

"No, I'm not a cockroach expert," he answered, annoyed. "I read a book about them."

"You read dumb things," Chris said. "You're always reading dumb books."

"Stop that kind of talk," scolded Mama. "Mark Charles can read what he wants to read. What he just told us is interesting. I didn't know all that stuff about cockroaches and neither did you. But I still don't want them in my kitchen, just like I don't want flies or mosquitoes or any kinds of bugs.

"We're going to have to ask the super to spray, especially Mrs. Glicklik's apartment downstairs. You know your Mama never likes to say anything bad about people, but that woman lives like a pig. The cockroach must have come up from her apartment. Her place is so filthy even the cockroach wouldn't want to live down there. Did Mr. Carlisle sense that something might be wrong, Mark Charles?"

"I don't think so, Mama, but I sure did. It was great that he asked us to go to the circus with him. He's nice to be with."

"He is pleasant," Mama said. "He has strong

facial features. You can tell a lot about people by looking at their faces. He has a confident face. He's not wishy-washy like a lot of people I've met, and believe me I've met a lot of people. Your Mama's a good judge of people—most of the time.

"Christopher Hugh, you start getting washed up and ready for bed now. Mark Charles and I will finish up the kitchen work. We can watch a little bit of the news together before we turn in."

"Why do I have to go first?" Chris asked.

"Because I told you to, that's why. When I tell you to do something, do it and don't question me about it. Remember, I'm your Mama. Now get into the bathroom and wash up. Now!"

9

"I *look like a clown!*"

Chris' eyes were the size of watermelons! He
didn't know where to look first. The razzle-
dazzle of the circus astounded him. Several
times he almost leaped right out of his seat.

"What's next, Mr. Carlisle?" he asked, as the
clown parade finished.

"Let's see," he answered, looking at the large,
colorful circus program. "Michu's on next—in
the center ring. He's one of the smallest men
in the world. He's only thirty-three inches tall
and weighs only twenty-five pounds. Here he
comes now," Mr. Carlisle said, pointing to the
entranceway. "He's on the third horse, the one
with the purple-spangled blanket."

"Gosh, he sure is tiny," Chris said. "Isn't he small, Mama? I'm bigger than he is, aren't I, Mama?"

"You sure are, son."

"Years ago," Mr. Carlisle continued, "there was a man called Tom Thumb who was the smallest man in the world. He was thirty-nine inches tall. Michu's smaller by six inches."

"I'm glad Michu's only thirty-three inches tall," Chris said.

"Why?" asked Mr. Carlisle.

"It's easier to remember," he answered. "Thirty-three's the number of our apartment. I can remember that easily when I tell my class at Wonderland about him."

"He has a quick mind," Mr. Carlisle said, turning to Mama.

"Very quick," she answered, smiling.

The crowd cheered Michu. Chris was fascinated with him. He couldn't believe anyone could be that small and still be a grown-up man.

When he came into the center ring, the lights dimmed, giving the audience the cue to start waving their circus flashlights around their heads. The stadium was a blaze of multicolored lights. As Michu rode off, the bright houselights came on again.

The ringmaster shouted: "AND NOW ABOVE YOUR HEADS, FOR THE FIRST TIME ANYWHERE IN THE WORLD, EXHILARATE WITH THE ADMIRABLY AMBITIOUS AERIAL ABRACADABRA

ASTUTELY ARTICULATED BY DANUTA, RING-
LING BROTHERS, BARNUM & BAILEY'S VERY
OWN SPIDER LADY, AS SHE PERFORMS WON-
DROUSLY IN HER AERIAL WEB!"

The crowd gasped as she spun around and
around on a shiny steel web, sometimes only
holding on with one leg, spinning so fast Chris
became dizzy. The audience cheered her performance.

"I never saw anything like it," Chris said.
"Isn't she great, Mama?"

"She sure is. She takes your breath away."

"What's that pink stuff on a stick?" Chris
asked, pointing to a vendor weaving in and out
among the seats.

"That's cotton candy," Mama answered.

"Yuck!" Chris exclaimed. "Candy made out
of cotton? The circus sure has surprising things."

Mr. Carlisle laughed. "It's called cotton candy
because it looks like cotton. It's made from spun
sugar. Haven't you ever had cotton candy?"

"No, sir," Chris answered.

"It's sweet and sticky," Mark said. "I had it
once at an amusement park when I was little."

"Would you like to try some?" Mr. Carlisle
asked. "Is it all right if he has some, Trudy?"

"I usually try to keep my boys off too many
sweets," she answered, "but since we're here
circusing, I suppose it's all right."

"Would you like one, Mark?" asked Mr. Carlisle.

94

"Yes, thank you," he replied.

Mr. Carlisle waved to the vendor. "Four, please," he told him, paying for the cotton candy.

"Four?" Mama asked.

"Well, you don't think the boys are going to have a circus treat and not us, do you? Here, Chris, Mark," he said, handing the big balls of fluffy cotton candy to them. "Pick it off the paper cone with your fingers and eat it like this," he told Chris, picking a chunk off the paper cone and eating it.

Chris took a piece of it and put it into his mouth. "Yum, it's good," he said. "But it disappears in my mouth so fast. It also makes my tongue feel prickly all over."

"That's from the sugar," Mama said. "It is good. I haven't had cotton candy for so long I almost forgot what it tasted like."

"The elephant parade is next," Mr. Carlisle said. "After that there'll be a fifteen-minute intermission."

"Inter-what?" asked Chris, picking away at the cotton candy.

"Inter*mission*," Mr. Carlisle answered. "That means there'll be a break before the second part starts."

"I don't want one," Chris said. "Can't it just go on?"

"The fifteen minutes will go by quickly," Mr. Carlisle told him. "Three hours is a long time

95

to sit without a break. The intermission will give us a chance to stretch our legs a bit. Look! Over there! The elephants are being lined up. Look!"

Mama laughed. Mr. Carlisle was just as excited as the boys were.

"Here they come," he cried. "Let's count them."

Chris couldn't have counted them if he'd wanted to. It was all too exciting. Dozens of the huge beasts stomped around the ring, covered with beautiful red-and-gold blankets with hundreds of glistening beads attached to them.

"AND NOW," the ringmaster shouted, "THE GREATEST SHOW ON EARTH TREKS TO THE TRANSFIXING TROPICS IN A TUMULTUOUS THREE-RING TRIBUTE TO THE CAPTIVATING CARIBBEAN! ELEGANT EDUCATED ELEPHANTS PROVIDE A PULSATING PROFUSION OF PACHY-DERMIC PAGEANTRY. FOR THE FIRST TIME ANY-WHERE—HERE IS THE ELEPHANT CALYPSO!"

As the band began to play, the elephants danced to the rhythm of a rhumba.

"Spectacular," Mama said. "It's just spectacu-lar! I've got goose bumps all over my body. Can you imagine getting goose bumps from a pack of elephants dancing the rhumba? What a circus this is!"

"It's unbelievable," Mark agreed.

They all had their eyes riveted to the sight.

As the elephants began parading out from the ring, the houselights came on.

Mama looked at Mark, Chris, and Mike and began laughing so hard, tears came from her eyes.

"You should see yourselves," she said between laughs. "All three of you are covered with pink from the cotton candy. You look like clowns! Here, look, Mike," she said, taking her compact mirror from her pocketbook.

"Mama, you'd better look in your mirror, too," Mark said, laughing.

Her lips were also covered in pink. They all laughed at themselves and at one another. Mike took a tissue from his pocket and began wiping her lips. The cotton candy was still so sticky that the tissue stuck to her.

"We'd better go and wash our faces," he said.

Still laughing, she said, "Mike, take the boys to the men's room. I'll go to the ladies' and we'll meet outside."

"We won't miss anything, will we, Mr. Carlisle?" Chris asked. "I don't want to miss one single thing."

"No, we have plenty of time. The intermission lasts fifteen minutes. Intermissions are good for getting sticky cotton candy off your face," he said, laughing.

"Come along, boys," Mama said, peering into her mirror and laughing. "*I* look like a clown!

All of us do. Why, if that ringmaster sees us, he'll put us into one of the acts."

"I'd like to be a clown when I grow up," said Chris. "A clown in this circus."

"There's nothing wrong with being a clown, but your Mama has other plans for you," she answered.

Climbing the stairs to the exit, she said, "I'm having the time of my life, Mike. So are the boys. I can't remember when we've had so much fun."

"I'm having a great time, too, Trudy," he answered, taking her hand and squeezing it gently. "It's the best time I've had in a long, long while."

Chris babbled on and on about the night.

"We really should try to go to sleep," Mark said. "It's late. Mama's already sleeping."

"I don't think I'll ever be able to sleep again," Chris said. "Every time I close my eyes, I see the circus. I can even still hear the music in my head. This was the best night of my life."

"It was fun," Mark said. "It sure was nice of Mr. Carlisle to take us to the circus."

"I think he likes us," Chris said. "I know he likes Mama."

"Why do you say that?" asked Mark.

"Because he was holding her hand," he said, giggling. "I saw them holding hands when the lights came up."

"Do you like him?" Mark asked.

"I sure do," Chris replied. "He's great."

Mark thought so too. "Good night, Chris," he said, plumping up his pillow with his fist.

"Night, Mark," Chris answered back. "Sometimes I wish I could keep nights like this alive forever and ever."

10

"When we say we'll clean it, we mean it!"

"Hi, Mama," Mark said, coming into the laundry.

"Hi, honey. Where's Christopher Hugh? Didn't he come along with you?"

"He stopped by next door for a minute. He wanted to look at the parrot in The Paradise Pet Shop. He'll be right here. Where's Mr. Jacobs?"

"He went next door to the luncheonette to grab a quick sandwich. We were quite busy all day."

"Can I help with anything, Mama?"

"No, everything's under control. Don't the decorations look nice?"

"Real nice," Mark replied, looking up at the

orange and green streamers attached to the fluorescent lights.

"This is a big occasion for Mr. Jacobs," Mama said.

"How many people will come, Mama?" Mark asked.

"There's no way of telling, son."

"The sign is a little small, isn't it Mama?" he asked, looking at the pint-sized poster on the cash register that read:

OPEN HOUSE
COME CELEBRATE
THE 15TH ANNUAL ANNIVERSARY PARTY
SATURDAY—JUNE 8TH—6:00–7:30
REFRESHMENTS AND SURPRISES!

"It's big enough for the customers to see, Mark Charles. Besides, Mr. Jacobs put an announcement in last night's *Citizen Dispatch*. Look, here it is," she said, showing him the newspaper.

"What are the surprises?" he asked.

"I'm glad you asked me that now, while Mr. Jacobs isn't here. He's so upset he could die! He planned on giving everyone two surprises: a balloon with his name and telephone number on it, which you and Christopher Hugh can help blow up later, and a special personalized key chain. The balloons came but the key chains didn't. If they don't come in this afternoon's mail, which should have been here by now, he'll be so disappointed. Both the balloons and the key chains were ordered over a month ago from the same company. He called about the key chains this morning and they promised they'd arrive. But there's no guarantee.

"The post office these days is a disgrace. An absolute disgrace. Why, it takes longer for a package to get across town than it does to go to Africa!"

"Hi, Mama," Chris called, dashing into the laundry. "Mama, the parrot talked to me."

"What did he say, son?"

"He said, 'What's your name?' When I told him Chris, he answered, 'Kiss. Kiss.' That's some funny bird, Mama. I'd love to have a parrot like that for a pet. Do you think someday I can have one, Mama?"

"You can have one when you grow up and have a place of your own. I don't like birds in the house. I never did. I especially don't like big birds like parrots. They need constant care. Besides, they're very dirty birds. When God made parrots, He put them in the jungle where they belong. He didn't put them on earth to be cooped up in a cage in an apartment. God knew what He was doing."

"Shucks! I'd love a parrot like that," Chris said.

"Mama wants you to have everything you want in life," she answered, "except a parrot! I don't want to hear any more about that bird now. I'm busy. Mark Charles, stay out here in front for a while and call me if a customer comes in. Christopher Hugh, you come in the back with me. You can open up the packages of paper plates and cups for tonight's party. That'll be a big help."

About five minutes later, Mark called, "Mama, the mail just came. There's a big box here. It might be the key chains."

She dashed to the front of the store. Quickly opening the box, she said, "It *is* the key chains. It's a miracle. A post office miracle. Christopher Hugh," she called.

"Yes, Mama," he answered, coming from the back.

"Do me a big favor, son, and go and tell Mr. Jacobs the key chains came."

"Key chains?" he asked.

"Yes, key chains. They're one of the surprises for tonight's anniversary party. Oh, he'll be so excited. Go and tell him, son. Now."

Chris began walking back to the door that led downstairs.

"What are you doing?" she asked. "Where are you going? I just told you to go and tell Mr. Jacobs that the key chains came."

"I am," Chris answered. "I'm going downstairs to tell him."

"He's not downstairs. He's next door at the luncheonette."

"How am I supposed to know that?" he asked. "I thought he was downstairs. I'm not a mind reader, you know."

"That last part was sassy, son. Quite sassy! I don't want you to have a sassy tongue—ever—especially with me. Now go over to the luncheonette and tell Mr. Jacobs the key chains came."

Chris left.

Within minutes Mr. Jacobs rushed in, with Chris trailing behind. "I never thought they'd come in time for tonight's party."

"It's a good sign," Mama said, "a sign that the party is going to be a big success."

"They're even nicer than I thought they'd be, Trudy," he said, proudly examining the key chains. "Here," he added, taking three key chains out of the box, handing one to each of them. "I want you to have the first ones."

"Thanks," Mark said, wondering why they were both so excited over a plastic key chain. He wasn't.

"That's very kind of you, Mr. Jacobs," Mama told him. "Thank you."

"Thanks," Chris said. "What is it?"

"Can't you see it's a key chain?" she answered. "It's to put keys on."

"I know that, Mama, but what is this thing attached to the chain?"

"It's a little bottle of bleach, son."

"What does it say on it?" he asked.

"On the front," she answered, "it gives Mr. Jacobs' name and telephone number. On the back it says, 'When we say we'll clean it, we mean it!'"

104

"That's so clever, Trudy," said Mr. Jacobs. "Your mother thought that slogan up," he told the boys. "I'd never think of anything that clever if I lived to be a hundred years old."

"Thank you, Mr. Jacobs," she said, pleased he was so happy. "I was always good making up rhymes. I used to write a lot of rhymes when I was a girl. My eighth-grade teacher told me she thought I'd grow up and become a poet someday. A poet—like Carl Sandburg or Robert Frost. English was always one of my best subjects."

"Speaking of English," Mr. Jacobs said to Mark, "you did a damned good . . ."

"Mr. Jacobs!" Mama exclaimed.

"I'm sorry, Trudy," he said. "It slipped out. You did a *darned* good job with the interview with Mike Carlisle. Your mama showed it to me last Wednesday."

"Thanks, Mr. Jacobs," Mark said, beaming.

"Mike thought so, too," she said. "Everyone I showed it to thought so."

"Everyone seemed to like it except Teddy," Mark replied.

"Who's Teddy?" asked Mr. Jacobs.

"A boy in my class," Mark answered. "He told me it stinks."

"Well, he was just jealous," Mama said. "Jealous that you got to do it in the first place and jealous that it was so good. Remember what I told you once—what Abraham Lincoln said: You can please some of the people some of the time, but you can't please all of the people all of the time. He was right. He was a smart man. Probably the smartest President we ever had. If Mike was pleased, and he was the interviewee, don't be concerned what Teddy said.

"Now I think we'd better check to see if everything's in order for the party. Come along, boys. Come with me to the back room and we can start blowing up the balloons. The party will be starting before we know it. We have a lot of blowing to do."

"I thought I'd come a little early," Mr. Carlisle said, entering the laundry, "just in case you needed some help."

"Thanks, Mike," Mama said, "but everything's all set."

"Hello, Mike," Mr. Jacobs called, appearing from the back room. "How are you?"

"Great, Jeremiah," he answered. "Congratulations on your fifteenth year. Here," he said, carefully handing him a plastic shopping bag. "I brought you a gift. I thought you'd like an orchid to put in the window. It's the perfect light for it."

"Thank you very much, Mike," Mr. Jacobs said, taking the orchid out of the bag. "This is some beauty. I only hope I can give it proper care."

"I'll take care of it for you," Mama said. "It's

106

a *Phalaenopsis.* They're as easy to take care of as plastic! I have two at home that Mike gave me. I never thought I'd be able to grow anything as beautiful as real, live orchids. Never in my entire life. Mike got me hooked on them. We can put the orchid on the refreshment table and use it as a centerpiece."

"You did a fantastic job with the decorations, Trudy," Mike said.

"They do look nice, don't they?"

"If nothing else," Mr. Jacobs said, "it's the prettiest party this place has ever seen. Mike, come give me a hand. I want to bring a table out here."

As Mama was fixing one of the streamers that was tumbling down, Mrs. Rand walked in.

"My goodness," she said. "Am I the first one to come to the party?"

"Oh, no, come on in, dear. Mike's here already. He's in the back with Mr. Jacobs and the boys."

"I rarely get to go to a party," said Mrs. Rand. "I'm so delighted to be invited."

"You look very pretty, Mrs. Rand. That print dress looks so good on you."

"I haven't worn it in over a year. I don't have much opportunity to get all gussied up and get out anymore. Here, darlin'," she said, handing Mama a big, rectangular box. "I baked some cupcakes this mornin' for the party. Two dozen. I hope they're enough."

107

"Why, Mrs. Rand, you didn't have to do that. You didn't have to bring anything at all. But thank you just the same."

"I couldn't come empty-handed. Not to an anniversary party."

"Hi, Mrs. Rand," Chris said, coming from the back.

"Hello, honey," she answered.

"You look pretty," he said to her.

"My goodness. Am I ever glad I came, even if I am early. That's two pretties I got right in a row!"

"Mama, Mr. Jacobs wants you."

"I'll be right back, Mrs. Rand. Sit down right here and make yourself comfortable," Mama said, leaving the front of the store.

As soon as she left, a man walked in carrying an armload of shirts. "Is Mrs. Kipness here?" he asked Chris.

"Yes, Mrs. Kipness is my mama," he answered.

"Then you must be Mark's brother."

"Yes, Mark's my brother. Who are you?"

"I'm Dr. Chrystal. I work at P.S. six eighty-six. Will you tell your mother I'm here?"

"Sure. I'll be right back," Chris answered.

"Why, Dr. Chrystal!" Mama exclaimed, quickly coming out front.

"I hope I'm not too late," he said.

"Oh, no. You're right on time. The party's just beginning."

"Party?" he asked.

108

"Didn't you come for the party? Tonight's Mr. Jacob's fifteenth anniversary party."

"No, I didn't know about that," he said. "These shirts have been piling up and I thought I'd bring them in."

"Just put them down on the counter," she told him. "I'll give you a ticket in a minute. I'll have them ready for you on Tuesday afternoon. Once you see how clean and fresh they'll be, you'll want to come here forever. I just know you'll be a regular customer. Mr. Jacobs isn't celebrating his fifteenth year for nothing, you know. This place has a good reputation and we intend to keep it that way—always!"

At that moment, Mr. Carlisle and Mr. Jacobs came out with the table.

"Mike!" Dr. Chrystal exclaimed. "I didn't expect to see you here."

"I'm surprised to see you, too," he said. "This is Mr. Jacobs, the owner. It's his party we're celebrating tonight. And this is Mrs. Rand," he added. "How's my favorite lady tonight?"

"I'm wonderful, Mike," she answered. "As wonderful as can be. Congratulations, Mr. Jacobs."

"Since you're here, Dr. Chrystal, why don't you stay for the celebration?"

"Thank you," Dr. Chrystal said. "I think I will."

He had never been to a party at a laundry before. Mrs. Kipness is quite a character, he thought. He also wondered what Mike was doing here.

Within a half hour the place was bursting. Mr. Jacobs was shocked to see so many people come. It was the biggest turnout in his fifteen years of business.

As Mama was pouring punch into little paper cups, she heard a familiar voice call, "Trudy! It's me!"

"Well, as I live and breathe!" she exclaimed. "Dotty Schmidt! I never expected to see you here."

"I decided to come at the last minute." Turning to Mr. Carlisle, she said, "You must be Mike Carlisle. I must say you look a lot more handsome in person. That photograph didn't do you justice."

"Photograph?" he asked.

"Yes, Trudy sent me the interview Mark did on you. It was a lovely piece."

"How did you know about the party, Dotty?" Mama asked.

"When you sent me the clipping, you included a note about it, remember?" she asked.

"Oh, that's right," Mama answered.

"Here's a bag of candy for the boys. I brought them an assortment—gumdrops, chocolate kisses, and some red and black licorice sticks."

"Thanks, Dotty, but you didn't have to do this. Let me pay you for the candy."

110

"That's ridiculous," Dotty answered. "Consider it a treat from me."

"Dotty, I'd like you to meet Dr. Chrystal. He works with Mike at P.S. six eighty-six. He's a doctor-psychiatrist. Dr. Chrystal, this is Dotty Schmidt. We worked together at the five-and-ten-cent store."

"Since everyone seems to be on a first-name basis, call me Nelson," he said to Dotty. "You too, Mrs. Kipness."

"Then you call me Trudy," she said.

"It's a pleasure to meet you," Dotty told him. "Where are the boys, Trudy?"

"I don't know. I guess they're lost in the shuffle," she said, looking around the crowded room for them. "Or they might be downstairs. They'll pop up soon. Come and have some refreshments, Dotty. I'll pour you some punch. I'm still flabbergasted that you came. What a surprising night this is. Surprising and fun."

11

"Why are you going around barefooted at a party?"

"I'm bored to death," Chris said. "It's so crowded upstairs. What are you reading?"

"A book about camels," Mark answered. "It's interesting. Did you know that if you're lost in a desert, dying from thirst, you could kill a camel and drink the water in its stomach?"

"Who cares?" Chris said. "That's disgusting! I wish there was a television set down here. I'm tired of all those people congratulating Mr. Jacobs. If I hear it one more time I'll scream!"

"The party will be over in about an hour. Be patient. Mr. Carlisle said he'd take us to Carvel on the way home. That'll be fun, won't it?"

"It will if it ever comes," Chris answered. "I

wish I had something to do," he said, gazing at a heavy-duty washing machine.

"I think I'll run the washing machine. I can watch the soapsuds spinning around through the glass door."

"You can't run an empty washing machine."

"I'll put this rag in it," he said, picking up a torn piece of towel. "It's dirty anyway. It'll come out nice and clean."

"I don't think you should be fooling around with the washing machine," Mark said. "Mama wouldn't like it."

"She won't care," Chris answered. "She's too busy pouring punch."

Chris put the rag into the washing machine, closed the door, and pushed a button. The machine began to whir and tumble.

"Where does the detergent go?" Chris asked, picking up a huge bottle of liquid detergent.

"In here," Mark said, pointing to a tiny hole at the top of the machine.

Chris unscrewed the cap of the plastic bottle of liquid detergent and poured some into the hole. He sat down on the floor, watching the suds mix in with the water. Mark went back to finish his book on camels.

Chris was fascinated with the rag rolling around. He tried to keep track of it as it tumbled through the suds. He then decided to add more liquid detergent, pouring more of it into the hole.

"Look at all the suds," he called to Mark. "It's better than watching a blizzard."

"Chris!" Mark said. "Please be quiet. I'm reading about how camels can live in temperatures as low as twenty degrees below zero. I never knew that. It's more interesting than your silly soapsuds."

"Sorry," Chris said, thinking the blizzard was just as interesting as the stupid camel book.

I think I'll pour some more in, Chris thought, pouring more detergent into the hole.

Within a few minutes soapsuds slowly began to leak from the washing machine door.

"I think I put too much in," Chris called. "It's leaking out a little."

Mark put down his book and went over to the washer. "You'd better wipe off the door with some paper towels," he said, handing Chris a large roll of Bounty.

Chris began wiping, but more and more suds continued to leak out. Soon, suds began dripping from the door onto the floor.

"I think we're in trouble," Chris said, wiping away. "Maybe we'd better stop this thing."

"*We're* not in trouble," Mark said. "*You're* in trouble. I didn't do anything."

"I really think we'd better stop the machine," said Chris.

"We can't stop it. It has to run its cycle."

"Can't we pull out the plug?" asked Chris.

"I don't know where it is," Mark answered.

114

"It's connected to one of those," he said, pointing to a jumble of wiring and plugs alongside the washing machine. "The suds should go out when it goes on the rinse cycle."

"The rinse cycle better come fast," Chris said. "Yuck! My hands are getting slippery."

Suds kept leaking and leaking. Mark and Chris kept wiping them up at a furious pace.

"If Mama comes down, she's going to kill us," Mark said. "Look at the mess you made."

"I didn't make a mess," Chris answered. "The dumb machine is doing it."

"If you hadn't turned it on in the first place, we wouldn't have had this mess," Mark said. "I'm going to see if there's a rag or mop around. It'll be easier than using these paper towels. Keep wiping!"

"Mark!" Chris yelled. "You'd better come back—and fast!"

Mark dashed back. Soapsuds began covering the floor. Chris kept moving back so he wouldn't step in them. Mark took the mop and tried to push them back. It was no use. Suds were pouring from the washing machine like a volcano erupting.

"We're going to get killed," Mark said. "This is terrible. Soap's all over the place. If this doesn't stop soon, we're going to drown in them. Take off your sneakers and socks," he told Chris, quickly untying his own shoelaces.

"Boys!" Mama called.

"We're through!" Mark said, frantically trying to push the suds back. "This is it. It's all over for us."

"Boys?" she called again. "I'd like you to come upstairs and enjoy the end of the party. Mr. Jacobs is going to pass out the surprises soon."

If either Mama or Mr. Jacobs walked downstairs at this very moment, they'd pass out themselves, Mark thought. "Go upstairs," he told Chris. "Tell her I'll be right up. Don't let her come down here or it's the end of us!"

"What'll I tell her?" Chris asked.

"Tell her I'm reading and I'll be up as soon as I finish a chapter."

"That's a lie," Chris said. "I can't lie to Mama."

"*This* time you can," he said. "Would you rather be caught telling a little lie or be dead? If this doesn't stop soon you'll be dead and buried in soapsuds. We both will be!"

"Coming, Mama!" Chris shouted, racing up the stairs.

From the doorway, he saw Mama standing near the punch bowl. Going over to her, he said, "Mark will be right up. He's finishing a chapter of his camel book."

"Do you want some more punch?" she asked.

"No, thanks, Mama. But I'll take a cup down to Mark."

"He can come up and have some."

"He wants some now," he said. "Reading about camels in the desert made him thirsty.

116

He'll come right up for more, as soon as he finishes his chapter."

As she handed him the cup of punch, she asked, "Christopher Hugh, why are your hands so wet?"

"I washed them," he answered sheepishly.

"Well, when you wash, you should dry," she said, handing him a paper napkin. Then, startled, she asked, "Where are your socks and sneakers? Why are you going around barefooted at a party?"

"My feet were hot. I took them off."

"That's ridiculous. Put them right back on. And tell Mark Charles I want him to come up. Now! Dotty Schmidt's here. She brought the two of you a nice bag of candy. I want both of you to thank her—with your socks and sneakers on, you hear?"

Chris took the cup of punch and raced to the stairway. Walking halfway down, he saw Mark standing in soapsuds up to his ankles, mopping away frantically. The floor was covered. You could hardly see any of the floor because of the bubbly mountain of suds continuing to stream out of the washing machine.

"Oh, boy!" Chris exclaimed. "What are we going to do? I'm scared!"

"Don't come down," Mark said, trying to roll up his dungarees with one hand. "Go and get Mr. Carlisle. Don't say anything to Mama. Just tell him to come down—and fast!"

117

Still holding the cup of punch, Chris fled back upstairs. He carefully looked around the room. He saw Mama talking to a woman. He looked around for Mr. Carlisle. He was standing, talking to Mrs. Rand. He made a dash toward him, praying that Mama wouldn't see him.

"Mr. Carlisle," he said, tugging at his sleeve, all out of breath. "Come downstairs—fast! Mark wants you."

"What does he want?" he asked.

"Why are you goin' around barefooted?" Mrs. Rand commented.

"My feet are hot," he said quickly. "Mr. Carlisle, please come. *Please! Now!*"

Mr. Carlisle sensed something was wrong.

"I think I'll come along, too," Mrs. Rand said. "It's gettin' a little stuffy up here. The cellar must be cooler. Besides, I've never been downstairs. This is my opportunity to see where your Mama spends most of her time."

"You can't!" Chris exclaimed. "I mean it's hot down there. It's hotter than a desert. That's why I took my socks and sneakers off. Here," he said, handing her the cup of punch Mama had poured for Mark. "Drink this. It'll make you feel cooler. Please, Mr. Carlisle. Come down," he pleaded, tugging again at his shirt sleeve, pulling him away from Mrs. Rand. "We're in trouble, Mr. Carlisle," he said. "A lot of trouble."

Halfway down the stairs, Mr. Carlisle saw

Mark standing in a pond of suds, holding the mop.

"Good Lord above! What happened?" he asked. "What did you do?"

Mark didn't answer. He was so frustrated he felt like crying.

Quickly, Mr. Carlisle began removing his shoes and socks, turning up his pants.

Drifting through the suds, he moved toward the washing machine and pulled out the plug. The machine stopped whirling and twirling immediately but the suds didn't. The entire floor kept bubbling away.

He searched to find the floor drain. It wasn't easy. When he finally found it, he pulled up the metal covering with his fingers. As soon as he did, some of the soapsuds slowly slushed down the drain.

"Grab that hose over there, Mark," he said. "I'll have to tease the suds down the drain. It's so bubbly that only a little bit can get down at a time. This is going to take a while."

"How long?" Mark asked.

"It could take at least two hours! Maybe more!"

"Mama's going to find out then, won't she?" Chris asked.

"She sure will," Mr. Carlisle answered.

"That blows Carvel!" Chris said.

"It sure does," Mr. Carlisle said.

119

"She's going to murder us," said Mark.

"I don't know how the two of you did this, but it sure was a stupid thing to do. Your mother has a right to be angry with you. What a mess you made down here!"

"She's going to murder us," Mark repeated.

"She might," Mr. Carlisle said, "and if you just keep standing still with that mop and repeating that phrase, I might just give you a good firm swat on your behind. You'd deserve that. Move that mop toward the drain while I run the hose. What an unbelievable mess you created. Trudy's going to have a fit!"

12

"Dotty Schmidt looked like a fallen Statue of Liberty."

"Yippee!" Chris shouted, racing toward the television dial. "It's nine o'clock!"

"Here, here! What are you doin'?" asked Mrs. Rand. "Don't you dare go turnin' on that T.V. set!"

"Why not? It's nine o'clock, isn't it?"

"What in the world does nine o'clock have to do with anythin'? You know what your mama said—no T.V. for a week for neither of you!"

"The week's up!" he exclaimed. "She told us that last Saturday night at nine o'clock. It's exactly one week now since Mama punished us for flooding the floor at the laundry. I remember it like it was a second ago. Can't I just watch one program before I go to bed, Mrs. Rand? Can't I? Please?"

"Absolutely not! That's somethin' for your mama to decide on. Besides, it's gettin' near time for you to get into your bed."

"If I don't watch at least one television show before I go to bed, I won't sleep the whole night," Chris said. "I'll be tossing and turning and thinking about television all night long."

"You'd better get ready for a sleepless night, then," she answered. "I'm not lettin' you turn on the T.V. set. And I don't want any more talkin' about it either. Calm yourself down. Go wash up and get your pajamas on. We're goin' to have some milk and chocolate cupcakes together before I turn you in."

"Aw, gee," Chris whined. "I've been punished enough. A week without watching television has been like starving to death. Mama wouldn't even let me see the news. How am I supposed to know what's going on in the world if I can't even watch a news program?"

"You could have listened to the news on the radio if you wanted to."

"That radio's crummy. All we get is static on it. You sure you won't change your mind, Mrs. Rand? I won't tell Mama."

"I know you won't, 'cause there's not goin' to be anythin' *to* tell her. Get in the bathroom!"

"Aw, gee," Chris whined again.

Although he knew better, he had thought she just might give in to him. Realizing it was hopeless, he slowly shuffled into the bathroom.

"Mark?" Mrs. Rand called. "Come into the kitchen. I'm puttin' our milk and chocolate cupcakes out. You can help me."

As he entered the kitchen, she said, "That little brother of yours just tried to con me into lettin' him watch T.V. He's gettin' to be quite a little devil these days."

"I still can't understand why I got blamed for flooding the floor," Mark said. "I didn't have anything to do with it. I was sitting downstairs reading this great book about camels when all of a sudden the suds came rushing out of the machine. It isn't fair that I should have been punished, too. Do you think it's fair, Mrs. Rand?"

"Well, you are older, Mark. And you were there while Chris was doin' it all. The least you could've done was to put your book down for a minute or so and go right upstairs and tell your mama. It might've saved a lot of unnecessary trouble."

"I still can't believe how angry Mama was. I never saw her get that mad before."

"She didn't stay mad for long," Mrs. Rand said. "She's not the kind of woman to hold a grudge against anybody, especially a grudge on you two boys."

Chris returned from the bathroom.

"You look nice and clean," said Mrs. Rand. "Sit down now and have your milk and cupcake."

"Will you play a game of Old Maid with me before I go to bed?" Chris asked Mark.

"No!" he exclaimed. "I told you I wouldn't play with you until Mama let us watch television again."

"Boy!" Chris said. "I feel just like a criminal. I get punished two ways. First by Mama, then by you. It's not fair."

"It's not fair that I had my television privileges taken away, either. Especially when I didn't do anything. It was all your fault and I got blamed for it."

"Do you think Mama will let us watch television tomorrow?" Chris asked.

"I guess she will," Mark answered. "The week's up tonight."

"The week's up right now," Chris said. "We should have asked her before she went to the movies. Will you play another game of Old Maid with me, Mrs. Rand?"

"Not tonight, Chris. That Old Maid is comin' out of my skin. I already got her four times tonight. I'm beginnin' to feel like an old maid myself."

"Is Dotty Schmidt an old maid?" Chris asked.

"Why do you bring her up?" Mrs. Rand asked.

"Well, she's never been married. Doesn't that make her an old maid?"

124

"That kind of talk isn't proper. It's all right to call a game Old Maid, but you don't go around callin' people that."

Chris began laughing.

"What are you laughing about?" Mark asked.

"Every time I think about Dotty Schmidt slipping in the suds and landing on her rear end, I laugh."

"That isn't somethin' to laugh about," Mrs. Rand said. "That poor woman could have gotten herself hurt."

"I know, but it's funny. Even Mama and Mr. Carlisle laughed about it last Sunday. She looked so funny sitting in the suds holding a mop over her head. I heard Mama tell Mr. Carlisle that Dotty Schmidt looked like a fallen Statue of Liberty."

"You certainly caused Mr. Jacobs' party to end with a bang," Mrs. Rand said.

"With a flood," said Mark.

"I still don't know why Mama punished us for a whole week," Chris said. "Mr. Jacobs even said it wasn't such a big deal."

Changing the subject, Mrs. Rand asked, "Do you like my cupcakes? I baked them fresh this mornin'."

"They're real good," said Chris, munching away. "Can I have another one, please?"

"I'll cut one in half. You shouldn't eat too much before goin' to bed. You'll have bad dreams. Do you want another half, Mark?"

125

"Thank you," he answered. "They are good."

"I've been usin' that recipe for as long as I can remember. Before you both were even born."

"What time is Mama coming home?" Chris asked.

"I don't know," Mrs. Rand answered. "She and Mike are goin' to stop off somewhere after. You'll be long sleepin' before she comes home."

"Mama and Mr. Carlisle have been going out a lot lately," Chris said. "I'm beginning to think she likes him better than she does us."

"That's a funny thing to say," Mrs. Rand said. "Your mama loves you both more than anythin' in the world."

"Then why does she spend so much time with Mr. Carlisle?" Chris asked.

"Because they get along together, that's why. Your mama and Mike make a nice couple. I've never seen her as happy as she's been these past few months. It's good for her to get out of the house once in a while. She works far too hard and long. She needs some recreation. Besides, Mike's very good to both you boys."

"I think Mama is in love with him," Chris blurted out between bites.

"That's none of your business," Mark said.

"It is so my business. She's my mama, too, isn't she? What if they do fall in love and Mama

126

marries him and she forgets all about us and puts us away in a home?"

"Your mind's spinnin' off some confusin' thoughts, son. Deep down inside that tiny body of yours, you know better than to think your mama or Mike would ever put you away. What gives you such a funny idea?"

"I saw a television show once where something like that happened. This lady married a guy and his daughter ran away because she wasn't wanted around anymore."

"That kind of thing might have happened on some T.V. show, but it won't happen here in real life to you. I just told you, and you know it as well as I do, that your mama loves you both more than anythin' in the world."

"Do you think they are getting serious about one another?" Mark asked.

"I'm beginnin' to suspect there's somethin' there between them. Somethin' very special. I also think it's the best thing that's happened to your mama in a long time. A woman's whole life shouldn't be spent lovin' only her children. There's different kinds of lovin'. Your mama has enough love to give the two of you to last forever and still have a lot left over. I think Mike does, too. He's a lovin' kind of man.

"Mark, you know I believe that lovin' has the power to change things. I believe that. I believe that so much. Lovin' can change things for the best even though it may not seem to be for the best at the time it's happenin'."

"Isn't Mama too old to fall in love?" asked Chris.

"You're never too old to love someone, son. You'll find that out as you grow up and get as old as I am. It's the love I have in my heart for my husband Eli, may he rest in peace, that keeps me goin' through life. Even though he's been dead and buried for five years now, all I have to do is glance over at his picture, or feel the pocket watch he carried with him all the time, and the memories of our love come right back to me. Love can be so strong that not even death can take it away from you. And it makes life a lot easier when it's around."

"I hope Mama's not getting too crazy about him," Chris said.

"You're crazy for even saying such a thing," Mark said.

"You're crazier than I am!" snapped Chris. "I think everyone's getting crazy around here."

"Here, here! I think this is enough talk for now," Mrs. Rand said. "It's not fittin' for two brothers to call one another any kind of names. Now both of you are goin' to brush your teeth and get into your bedroom. I want to read the newspaper—in peace. Chris, go brush your teeth first while Mark and I clean up."

"Shucks!" Chris said. "All I do is get yelled at around here—by everybody! Maybe I'll run

128

away like the girl on television did. Then everyone will be sorry."

"The only place you're goin' to run to is into the bathroom," said Mrs. Rand. "Now get!"

"What in the world are you doing now?" Mark asked, looking over at Chris, who was sitting up in bed.

"Nothing," he answered, sneakily sliding his hands under the cover.

"You're doing something," Mark said.

"I'm not doing anything. I'm trying to see if I can sleep sitting up."

Mark knew he was up to something. He got out of his bed, walked over to Chris, and threw back the cover. Sitting on top of Chris' belly was a half-eaten cupcake.

"Where did you get that?" Mark asked.

"From the kitchen. Where do you think I got it?"

"Mrs. Rand told you you couldn't have another cupcake. And you shouldn't be eating that thing in bed. You'll have crumbs all over the sheets."

"It's my bed, isn't it?" he said. "If I want to sleep in crumbs, it's my business."

"You won't feel that way when the cockroaches start crawling all over your body," Mark said, taking the cupcake and throwing it into the wastebasket. "You'd better get to sleep now. Boy, if Mama came home and saw you doing this, she wouldn't let you watch television until you graduated from high school! Now try to sleep and have a good night."

"There's nothing good about tonight," Chris said.

"Well, tomorrow will be better. Mama will let us watch television again tomorrow."

"If things don't get better starting tomorrow, I'm going to run away," Chris said. "Just like the girl on television did and everyone will be sorry for picking on me. This has been the worst week of whole life. I'm beginning to hate it here!"

13

". . . but names
will never hurt me."

"It's beautiful here, Mr. Carlisle," Mark said, as they strolled along the winding stretch of sandy beach. "I can't believe all this water and sand is here, and it's only a few hours away from us."

"I can't believe you've never been to the sea-shore before," Mike said. "We'll have to come more often."

"Can we, Mr. Carlisle?"

"Only if you do me a favor," he answered.

"What's that?"

"I wish you'd start calling me Mike."

"Mama would have a fit if I called you by your first name, Mr. Carlisle."

"She wouldn't mind it if I said it was all right."

"You don't know Mama as well as I do, Mr. Carlisle. Even though you say it's all right, Mama would have to be the one to say so."

"I have an idea. Call me Mike when we're alone together, like this. It'll be a special kind of secret between us until I ask her about it. It's time both you and Chris dropped that Mr. Carlisle stuff. Do you agree?"

"I guess it's O.K. As long as Mama doesn't hear it. I know she'd have a fit, Mr. Car—"

"Mike!" said Mike.

"Look," Mark said, bending down to pick up a piece of small wood. "This looks like a fish, doesn't it?" he asked, holding the wood toward the bright light of the sun.

"It's a piece of driftwood, Mark. It does look like a fish."

"Driftwood?" Mark asked.

"It's called driftwood because it drifts on the ocean. See how it's weathered? The pounding of the waves and the constant washing of the salt water give it that look and texture."

"What do you think it was part of?"

"It could be anything—a part of an old tree, a boat, crate, or even a piece of wharf that drifted onto the sea."

"Can I keep it?" Mark asked.

"You sure can."

"Great! I'll put it on my bookshelf. It'll be my souvenir from here."

132

Mike laughed. "You really do like the shore, don't you?"

"I love it," Mark answered, squishing his toes into the warm, wet sand.

"Chris doesn't seem to like it very much," Mike said. "He's spent more time on the boardwalk this afternoon than on the beach."

"He doesn't like the sand on his body," Mark said. "It makes him feel icky all over."

"There are times, Mark, when I think he doesn't like me very much, either."

"He does, Mike. He likes you a lot."

"You sure of that?"

"I'm positive he does. I know it."

"Sometimes he acts a little strange when I'm around."

"He's just a little jealous of you sometimes, Mike. That's all. He's used to having Mama for himself. Since you met her, you've been spending a lot of time together. There are times when I miss Mama being home with us every night."

"Mark, you're old enough to know that I have strong feelings for your mother. I've strong feelings for the two of you, too. It's funny. I always wanted to have a family. When my wife, Emma, suddenly died, that hope went out the window. I didn't think I'd ever find anyone who could replace her in my life. Then, as if by magic, you came along. If it weren't for you and a leaky kitchen faucet," he said, smiling, "I might never have gotten to know you and Chris or your mother. It's funny how things happen in life."

"Do you love Mama?" Mark asked.

"Whew!" he exclaimed, wiping beads of sweat from his forehead. "That's a big question."

"I mean," Mark asked hesitantly, "do you love her enough to consider getting married?"

"We haven't talked together about that yet, Mark. It's a big decision to make, one that the four of us would have to think about carefully. How would you feel about it?"

"I don't know. Sometimes I think it would be great, and sometimes the thought of it scares me a little."

"I feel the same way, Mark. Believe me I do. I'm sure Chris and your mother have mixed feelings about it, too. It's a big life decision to make, one that will have to take time to work out. I share your feelings, Mark. Please know that I do.

"Hey look!" he said. "There's your little brother and Trudy. See them up there on the boardwalk? They're coming back. Let's go meet them back on the blanket so they won't think we've disappeared. Mark, thanks for talking with me. I enjoy our times alone together."

"Me too," Mark answered.

He took Mark's hand. Quietly, they walked back toward the beach blanket.

The rest of the July and August soared by. Neither Mark or Chris could remember a time when it had ever passed so quickly.

There was never a dull moment during the summer. Mike and Mama took them to places they had never been before. They spent a day at the Bronx Zoo, went to two baseball games at Yankee Stadium, and took several more trips to the New Jersey shore. There were also picnics, movie matinees on a few rainy Saturdays or Sundays, and a trip to Hartford, Connecticut, to visit Mike's mother.

The summer had cemented their relationship. They were inseparable; happier than four people could hope to be.

It seemed just like yesterday that school had ended, and here it was October, a month into a new school year.

School seemed quite different this year to Mark. It was the first time he had a man for a teacher, Mr. Glubok. There were other things that changed the atmosphere of the school, too: Dr. Chrystal, a regular customer now at Mr. Jacobs' Laundry, was very friendly, going out of his way to say hello frequently. And there was Mike, who for years had been only a custodian at the school, now a wonderful friend, part of the family's life.

Over the summer, he had convinced Mama that the boys should call him Mike.

"Mr. Carlisle seems so stuffy, Trudy," he said one night, driving them back from the shore. "We're together so much, I think it would be better if they called me, Mike. That 'Mr.' stuff makes me feel a lot older than I am."

"If you say so, Mike," she agreed, "it's all right with me. But *only* when we're doing things on a social basis. Remember, Christopher Hugh is going to be going to first grade at P.S. six eighty-six next month and I don't want him, nor Mark Charles, running around the school calling you by your first name—ever! That's your place of business. I want them to show respect for your position there."

He agreed. It was Mike outside of school and Mr. Carlisle inside—always!

There were so many things Mark and Chris liked about Mr. Carlisle, but the one thing that thrilled Mark most of all happened on the very first day of school. When he went into Mr. Carlisle's office, he immediately noticed that on the desk, the interview he had done with him for the school newspaper last spring was standing in a silver frame where the photograph of his late wife, Emma, had once stood. It made Mark feel ten feet tall.

"What are you going to be?" Chris asked Mark on the way home from school.

"What do you mean, what am I going to *be*?"

"For Halloween this year? What are you dressing up as?"

"I haven't thought about it yet," Mark said. "Halloween's still a few weeks away."

"That's all I've been thinking about," Chris said. "I love Halloween."

"How about being a ghost?" Mark asked.

"Ghosts are boring," Chris answered. "Anyone can be a ghost. I was thinking about being something exciting—like a space creature from Mars, or a fire-breathing dragon, or a . . ."

"I see you're baby walking again," a familiar voice interrupted from behind.

Mark turned around. It was Teddy.

"Who's he?" Chris asked.

"It's Teddy. A boy in my class. Hi," he said. "Teddy, this is my brother, Chris."

"Big deal," Teddy said. "I don't want to meet no baby."

"I'm not a baby!" Chris exclaimed. "I'm in first grade."

"You're a baby," Teddy said. "A shrimp. And your brother is a shrimpwalker."

"Look, bug off," Mark told him, standing at the corner, hoping the red light would change so they could get away from him.

"What are you, tough stuff?" Teddy asked.

"Just leave us alone," Mark said.

"What are you goin' to do if I don't? Tell the janitor I'm pickin' on you? I know all about him," Teddy continued. "He's got his eyes on your mother. My father told me he saw them at the movies together. What a combination! A janitor who cleans toilets and a lady who washes other people's dirty clothes."

"You leave my mother out of this," Mark said angrily.

"Yeah! Shut up about my mama," Chris added.

"You're a tough little baby shrimp," Teddy teased.

The light changed. Walking across the street, Teddy continued to follow them. "At least you'll always be clean," he said, "with a toilet cleaner and a washerwoman both around the house."

"I've had enough from you, Teddy," said Mark. "Bug off or I'll . . ."

"You'll do nothin'," Teddy interrupted. "You and that baby shrimp are two sissies. Sissy, sissy," he taunted, knocking Chris on the shoulder.

"Cut it out," Chris said. "And if you say one more thing about my mama or us . . ."

"Sissy, sissy. Sissy shrimp," Teddy chanted, continuing to tap Chris' shoulder.

Chris turned around and gave him a swift kick in the shin.

"Ow! I'll get you for that," Teddy screamed, grabbing Chris and throwing him down on the sidewalk.

Mark took Teddy's arm and twisted it around his back, squeezing so hard he couldn't move. "Say you're sorry or I'll break every bone in your arm," Mark said.

Chris got up from the sidewalk, somewhat dazed.

"I wouldn't say I'm sorry to you if you killed me," Teddy said.

138

"Say it!" Mark repeated, all out of breath.

Chris kicked him in the leg again.

"Ouch!" Teddy shouted. "I'm sorry. I'm sorry."

Mark let go of his arm.

"You're a skunk," Chris blurted. "A smelly skunk."

"Now leave us alone," said Mark.

"I sure will," Teddy replied. "You win."

Before walking away, he yanked at Chris' shirt, pulling it so hard he tore the front of it to pieces. He then fled around the corner, disappearing from sight.

Chris began bawling. "Look what he did, Mark. Look at my shirt. It's all ripped up. Mama's going to kill me."

"Stop crying!" Mark commanded, not believing what had happened. "Let's go home. Here," he said, handing Chris his pocket handkerchief. "Blow your nose and stop crying."

"Why did he do that?" Chris asked, blowing hard into the handkerchief. "We didn't bother him."

"He's mean," Mark answered. "He's the meanest person I ever met. No one likes him."

"What if he does it again?" Chris asked. "What if he attacks us tomorrow or the next day?"

"He won't do it again. I'm going to tell Mr. Glubok about this the first thing tomorrow. He'll make sure he gets punished for it. I'm not letting him get away with this."

"What will we tell Mama? She's going to kill me when she sees this shirt."

"Let's not tell her anything about this. Don't tell anyone. Let me handle it."

"He said nasty things about Mama and Mike. That's worse than his knocking me around and ripping my clothes off, isn't it, Mark?"

"Look, I'll take care of it. I promise. Forget about it. It happened and it's over with. When we get home, we'll throw the shirt down the incinerator."

"What'll I tell Mama?"

"I said not to tell her anything. If she does notice it's missing, tell her you took it to school—that it was old and you needed it for a paint smock."

"O.K.," he agreed, "but I don't like lying to Mama. If she ever catches me telling another lie after that soapsuds scene, my television privileges will go down the drain again. Maybe forever!"

They silently walked toward home.

Chris was right about Teddy's calling Mama and Mike names, thought Mark. Name calling hurt more than any shoving or ripping ever could.

Mama stormed through the door!

"Mark Charles! Christopher Hugh!" she called. "Are you in your room?"

"Yes, Mama," Mark called back.

"Get out here at once—both of you. At once, do you hear me?"

They quickly came into the kitchen.

"Hi, Mama," Chris said. "How was your day?"

"Don't you 'Hi, Mama' me. My day was super-fine until a half hour ago. What did the two of you do to that poor boy Teddy Cummings?"

"What?" Mark asked, shocked.

"*What* is what I want to know about," she answered. "Mrs. Cummings marched into the laundry with Teddy. That poor little thing was sobbing his heart out. He said the two of you attacked him on the street, and for no reason at all kicked him and twisted his arm. I can't believe it! You had better tell me all about this and fast, Mark Charles. And don't you dare leave out any details, either. Not one single little detail. I want to hear everything. Now sit down and talk!"

As Mark told her about the incident, Chris kept totally silent. He thought he'd die as Mark came to the end of the story, praying he would keep his promise and not mention the torn shirt, which they had already dumped down the incinerator. He didn't. Chris breathed a sigh of relief.

"Do you have anything to add, Christopher Hugh?" she asked.

"No, Mama. What Mark said is all true. Teddy was the one who started up with us. Really, he was."

"Well, I'm sorry I was so huffy when I came

141

in. I should have realized that my boys wouldn't do such a thing. It's not like either of you to be fighting in the middle of the street like hoodlums. When my nerves settle down, I'll call Mrs. Cummings and get this all straightened out. There are always two sides to every story, and she'd better know your side."

"That Teddy's a mean, smelly skunk," Chris said.

"Christopher Hugh! Do you want me to have a heart attack right here in the kitchen? You're name calling. You're as bad as that boy who had unkind things to say about Mike and me. There's an old saying that my great-grandmother, may she rest in peace, taught me when I was a young girl. It's older than the hills and you should know how it goes: 'Sticks and stones may break my bones, but names will never hurt me. When I die, you shall cry for all the names you called me.' "

"That's cute," Chris said.

"Cute? I know I'm going to have a heart attack from you. It isn't *cute*. It's a *message*. Don't you get the message behind that rhyme?"

"I didn't hit him with any sticks or stones," Chris said. "He's a liar. A liar and a . . ."

"Go right into your room and don't come out until I tell you to," she commanded.

"But . . ." Chris started to say.

"No buts. No talk. No more anything. Just get

142

into that room of yours or I'll do something I'll be sorry for later on."

"Chris!" Mark said.

"Boy!" Chris exclaimed, walking toward the bedroom. "He picks on us and I get punished. I'm always getting punished around here."

"I'm not punishing you, son. Just go. Go into your room and close the door behind you. I want to talk with Mark Charles."

Chris went into his room, closed the door, but left it open a crack to listen to what they were saying. He wanted to hear if Mark would spill the beans about the torn shirt. If he did, he might just as well leap out the bedroom window and end it all quickly, he thought. Mama would never forgive him for that, even if it wasn't his fault.

"Mike, it's Trudy here."

"Hi, I've been waiting for your call."

"I'm sorry I'm calling back this late, but I wanted to wait until the boys were asleep. It's been a rough day here."

"You sound tired out, Trudy."

"I am, Mike. I am tired out. I'm also a little unnerved with Christopher Hugh. He's starting to get the best of me."

"Aw, come on, Trudy. It was only a scrap. All boys get into a fight once in a while."

"It's not the fight, Mike. I'm convinced it

wasn't their fault. It's just that Christopher Hugh has been using some very strong language. And he's becoming more and more aggressive. He's been getting into a lot of mischief. If it's not one thing it's another. Last June he flooded the laundry, over the summer he broke the super's window with a homemade cardboard boomerang, and just last month, during the very first week of school, I had to meet with his teacher because he deliberately dipped Carrie Carmichael's hair into a jar of yellow paint! I never had such problems with Mark Charles. Ever!"

"There's a world of difference between Mark and Chris, Trudy. You know that. None of the things he did are so unusual. He's just a little mischievous. I think you're making too much of his behavior."

"You might be right, Mike, but I believe in getting to the root of problems before they grow into bigger ones. I won't tolerate his moods and I won't put up with his using bad language. If he's going to continue to be a fine boy, he'll have to put up with my rules. I am his mama, you know."

"I know that quite well," Mike said, "but I think you're putting things out of proportion with Chris. He's a great little guy.

"Look, if it will make you feel any better, why don't you go in and see Nelson Chrystal? After all, he is a psychiatrist—and a pretty good one at that. He might be able to give you some good advice."

"That's not a bad idea. I feel I can trust Nelson. I've certainly changed my mind about him since I first met him. He's really a regular guy when you get to know him. Mike, can you do me a favor and make an appointment with him for me next Monday after school?"

"I sure will. Now listen, don't concern yourself anymore about the boys—or today's fight. I really look forward to seeing you Saturday night."

"I do too," she answered.

"I'll call you tomorrow afternoon at the laundry. Sleep well."

"You, too, Mike," she said. "Good night."

"Good night, Trudy. Trudy?"

"Yes, Mike?"

"I love you."

"I love you, too, Mike," she said, squeezing the telephone receiver tightly. "Good night."

14

*". . . I have something to
tell both of you."*

Mike was right. The meeting with Dr. Chrystal
helped her understand Chris' behavior much
better.

"It's a natural state for a young boy to go
through," he told her. "He's uncertain about
many things. He just started a new school, which
makes many children feel a bit unsettled. More
important than that, Trudy, he may not be sure
of his relationship with you and Mike. Once he's
sure where the relationship is going, he'll calm
down a lot. Right now it's normal that he's a
little jealous. He probably feels Mike is taking
you away from him. That's why he's rebelling.

Remember, Trudy, Mark is older and has much more understanding than Chris could possibly have at this age."

It was all she had to hear. Throughout the next two weeks, she thought and thought about it. She talked with the boys, carefully trying to feel out their thoughts about Mike. She was pleased that they liked Mike so much.

The time had come to ask them. She had to.

"Mr. Jacobs?" she called downstairs. "Can you come up a minute? I have to call home."

"Be there in a second," he answered.

The telephone in the apartment rang.

"I'll get it," Chris said, running to the kitchen phone. "Hello, this is Christopher Hugh Kipness here."

Mama laughed. "I know it's you, son. I'd recognize your voice anywhere."

"I'm sorry, Mama," he said.

"About what?"

"If I knew it was you calling, I wouldn't have said my whole name."

"That's all right, son. How are you?"

"Fine, Mama."

"Good. Do me a favor and put your brother on the phone. I want to tell him something."

"O.K., Mama. Hold on."

He put the receiver down and ran into the living room. "Mark, Mama's on the phone."

147

"What does she want?" he asked.

"I don't know. She just said she wanted to talk to you."

"How does she sound?" Mark asked.

"Pretty good—for a Tuesday!"

Mark went to the phone. "Hi, Mama."

"Hi, son. Look, I'm a little busy. You know how busy Tuesdays are here, so I only want to talk for a minute or so. The reason I called is that Mike and I are going to take you both out to eat tonight."

"At the Burger Barn?" he asked.

"No, we're not going to the Burger Barn tonight. We're going to go a little fancy. We're taking you to Stella's Italian Kitchen, so dress up nice. Tell your little brother I want him to wear a clean shirt. His blue one."

"Is everything all right, Mama?"

"Everything is wonderful, son. Just wonderful. I know we don't usually eat out on Tuesdays, but the reason we're going to have supper out tonight is that Mike and I have something to tell both of you—something very interesting, and I hope something special—very special! Meet us at the laundry at six fifteen, O.K.?"

"O.K., Mama."

"Good-bye, now. Be sure and double lock the door, son."

"I will, Mama. Good-bye."

Hanging up the telephone, he called, "Chris!"

"Yes?"

148

"We're going out to eat tonight—at Stella's Italian Kitchen—with Mama *and* Mike. She said they want to talk to us about something very interesting and very special."

"You know what it is?" Chris asked.

"I think so. Do you?"

"Yes," Chris said, smiling. "I think Mama's going to tell us she's going to have *three* boys around the house soon—me, you, and Mike."

"How do you feel about it?" Mark asked.

"I like the idea," Chris answered. "I like it very much. It's about time!"